The Case of the EXPLODING BRAINS

RACHEL HAMILTON

SIMON AND SCHUSTER

First published in Great Britain in 2015 by Simon and Schuster UK Ltd
A CBS COMPANY

3 5 7 9 10 8 6 4 2

Simon & Schuster UK Ltd
1st Floor,
222 Gray's Inn Road
London WC1X 8HB

www.simonandschuster.co.uk

Simon & Schuster Australia, Sydney
Simon & Schuster India, New Delhi

A CIP catalogue record for this book
is available from the British Library.

PB ISBN: 978-1-47112-133-3
EBOOK ISBN: 978-1-47112-134-0

Printed and bound by CPI Group (UK) Ltd, Croydon, CR0 4YY

For my gorgeous godsons – Brad, Ollie and Eliot – whose parents are foolish enough to believe that I'm a responsible adult

1

Go Directly To Jail

Prison?

What am *I* doing in prison?

Prison! Jail! Clink! The slammer! The pen! (Hmm. Not sure about that last one. I read it in an American mystery novel, but it sounds more like somewhere you'd put sheep.)

Who'd have believed that I, Noelle 'Know-All' Hawkins, winner of Butt's Hill Middle School's Annual Achievement Award for the last five years, would end up visiting my father in prison?

I've been nervous about coming, particularly since Holly told me the iron in my multivitamin tablets might set off the metal detectors. I think she was joking but it's hard to tell with my sister. She also said I should watch out for fellow prison visitors carrying concealed weapons.

> **con·ceal** (kən-sēl´)
>
> *tr.v.* **con·cealed, con·ceal·ing, con·ceals**
> To keep from being seen, found, observed
> or discovered; to hide.

That doesn't make sense. If visitors are keeping their weapons from being 'seen, found, observed or discovered', I can hardly watch out for them, can I? Besides, being concealed strikes me a good thing in a weapon. I suspect most weapon-related problems start when people are forced to reveal them – say because some stupid prison alarm goes off.

WOWOWWOWOWOWOWOWOWOW

When the siren starts to wail, I'm at the front of the Prison Visitors' Centre queue, holding out the ID that proves I'm the daughter of celebrity scientist (and convicted exploder of public toilets) Professor Brian 'Big Brain' Hawkins. I dive to the ground and curl up into a ball. I can't make myself concealed-weapon-proof, but I *can* form a smaller target. Twelve is too young to die: I have things to do, dictionary definitions to read, imprisoned parents to visit . . .

As I peek from my safe, beetle-like position on the floor, a pair of shiny official-looking shoes approaches the metal detector and stops in front of the scuffed boots of the man who set off the alarm.

"Empty your pockets please, sir," Mr Shiny Shoes says. "No sudden movements."

Scuffed Boots Man reaches inside his mouldy raincoat and pulls out a pack of cigarettes, a ball of fluff and a round metal tin.

What's in the tin? What's in the tin?

Explosives? Mini hand grenades? Ninja throwing stars?

I press my lips together but a whimper escapes.

"You alright, pet?" Scuffed Boots Man opens his tin and crouches beside me. "Fancy a mint?"

"A mint?" I echo. "The tin's full of mints?"

Mints are good. Mints don't kill. Well, not unless you swallow too many and they block your wind-pipe. And these ones do look a bit furry.

"No. Thank you." I clamber to my feet and dust off my corduroy suit. "I had a big lunch."

"What are you doing, you silly girl?" Aunty Vera (a.k.a. Vigil-Aunty) grabs my arm and drags me back to the front of the queue. "Show the man your ID."

I avoid eye contact with the prison guard but I can hear him sniggering, even after he's buzzed me through two heavy-duty security doors.

An official pointy-finger directs us towards Table Eight. Vigil-Aunty unclenches her right fist and scowls at our visitor reference number. Every visitor is issued with one in order to prevent people who want to harm the inmates from entering the prison – which is ironic, because if anyone wants to hurt Dad it's Vigil-Aunty.

Holly gave Aunty Vera that nickname. A vigilante is someone who takes the law into their own hands to avenge a crime. And if the police hadn't arrested Dad for blowing up a portaloo, Aunty Vera would have vigil-auntie-d him good and proper for aban-doning Mum, Holly and me. She insisted on coming today, vowing she'd chain herself to the prison bars before she let "that flaming man" convince me he's innocent.

I thought about protesting, but I needed an accompanying adult, so here we are. While we wait for Dad, I read the list of rules stuck to the table.

1. Prisoners must remain seated at all times
2. Children must not run in the Visiting Hall
3. No chewing gum
4. No foul or abusive language
5. No visiting any other inmates
6. Nothing to be brought in.
7. Nothing to be taken out

Fine by me. Especially Rule 5.

The prisoners enter the Visiting Hall and scan the room for friends and family.

"Like caged Velociraptors hunting their prey," Vigil-Aunty murmurs. She's in the middle of a creative writing course and her task for the week is 'introduce similes into your life'. Unfortunately, this involves introducing similes into everyone else's life too.

"You're confusing Velociraptors with Utahraptors," I explain. "It's a common mistake. Velociraptors were only around a metre high, but they made them bigger in those old Jurassic Park movies so they'd be scarier ..."

I pause, distracted by the sight of Dad limping into the hall behind the Utahraptors. He's covered in purple bruises, and his red, swollen nose makes him look like a clown who's lost a fight.

"*Archimedes!*" I squeak. "What happened to him?"

Vigil-Aunty tuts. I'd like to think it's an expression of horror at Dad's battered appearance, but I suspect it's because she hates my habit of calling out the names of famous scientists at times of stress. It's hard to imagine anyone failing to feel sorry for Dad after seeing him like this, but Vigil-Aunty seems to be managing fine.

"Your limp would be more convincing if you could remember which leg was supposed to be hurt," she mocks as he approaches. "Who've you upset this time, Brian? You look like you've gone two rounds with a Veloci ... bah! ... Utahraptor."

Dad glances over his shoulder and whispers, "My fellow inmates objected to a documentary I filmed last year."

"Poor Brian," Vigil-Aunty says with mock sympathy. "Last year? Would that have been while you were trying to brainwash small children with your brain-ray inventions? Or while you were abandoning your family to blow up toilets?"

"I've apologised for that, Vera. Several times. I can't believe you're still going on about it."

"Several times? SEVERAL TIMES?" Vigil-Aunty is clearly on the verge of breaking Rule 4. "You could apologise a million times and I WOULD STILL BE GOING ON ABOUT IT!"

"Please don't shout! You'll get us thrown out." I put a hand on her arm and then turn back to Dad. "I can understand why Aunty Vera is angry, but I don't get why some old documentary would make the prisoners here want to hurt you?"

"It wasn't any old documentary." Dad closes his eyes. "It was the one where I identified a particular class of criminals with huge muscles and tiny brains."

"I remember!" I say. "You called them Neanderthugs!"

"Shh!" Dad lifts a finger to his lips, wincing as he pokes his swollen nose.

Heads swivel: heads attached to enormous, muscular bodies.

I lower my voice. "You said Neanderthugs tended to end up in prison because they were too stupid to cover their tracks."

"Turns out I was right," Dad mutters. "Most of them *are* in prison. With me. And most of them spent last Tuesday evening watching the documentary."

A huge human bicep lumbers past our table and 'accidentally' kicks Dad's chair out from under him. Dad's face hits the table. When he lifts it, he has a nose to rival Rudolph's.

"Neanderthug Number One," Dad mutters through swollen lips.

With a pang of guilt, I remember the moment during the Case of the Exploding Loo when I could have let Dad wriggle free to escape the police. Sadly, I can't travel back in time (yet). But perhaps I can fix things in the present. I jump up and grab Neanderthug Number One's arm, trying not to notice how small my fingers look beside his 'No Mercy!' tattoo.

"Stop hurting my d-dad," I stutter, aware we're breaking Rule 1 and possibly Rule 5. "He didn't mean to upset you and – blimey, aren't you big? – there must b-be a way he can m-make things up to you."

Neanderthug Number One studies me as if I'm something on the bristles of his toilet brush. "Want moon," he grunts eventually.

"Moon?" I repeat with an anxiety that comes from too much time spent reading the dictionary:

Moon (mōōn)

n.

1. The natural satellite of Earth.
2. A natural satellite revolving around a planet.
3. The bared buttocks. (*Slang*)

"Is this a bare buttocks thing?" I ask nervously.

"NO!" Neanderthug Number One's bellow thunders through the hall. "WANT MOON! MOON MAKE HELL RAIZAH STRONG."

"Mr Raizah may have a point." Vigil-Aunty says. "I've heard that crime rates soar during a full moon. So do hospital admissio—"

"Baloney!" Dad barks. "Idiot woman! Scientific research shows no link between criminal activity and phases of the moon."

9

"You're the idiot." Vigil-Aunty raises her voice to be heard over Dad's spluttering and thrusts her face in his.

They both rise to their feet, going chin-to-chin over Table Eight.

"Rule 1!" I remind them. "And it doesn't matter which of you is the idiot. Science or no science, what matters is Mr Hell Raizah *believes* the moon will make him stronger."

"WANT MOON!" Hell Raizah roars. "YOU GET MOON, I GET NICE."

2

The Great Museum Heist

Six Days Later

I'm the first to sense something's wrong on the LOSERS (Lindon-based Opportunities for the Superior Education of Remarkable Students) trip to the Science Museum. I scan the 'Exploring Space' gallery, trying to work out what tripped my 'uh-oh' switch.

I study the moon landers that dangle from the ceiling, hinting at shiny adventures in other places. Nope. Not them. Not the missile parts lurking in the background either. Something simpler has aroused my suspicions – something made of turquoise plastic.

I hate turquoise. Turquoise is the colour that connected all the sinister organisations during the Case of the Exploding Loo. I suppose you could say turquoise helped me, my sister Holly and our friend Porter crack the case; but it also landed Dad in jail, so the turquoise walkie-talkies make me uneasy. And they're not the only problem.

I've never been a fan of Remarkable Student Alexander. I don't like the way he keeps reminding everyone that LOSERS invited him to join back when the school only admitted the 'brightest and the best'. This is a dig at students like Holly, who weren't accepted until LOSERS was forced to relax its admissions policy after the science teacher blew up half the building and the headmistress (Porter's mum and Dad's evil sidekick) was accused of kidnapping and brainwashing children.

But LOSERS is still a good school. At least it *was* until it relaxed its admissions policy so far it admitted Smokin' Joe Slater – who got his nickname by spending break and lunch times lurking in the school toilets, smoking cigarettes he'd nicked from his mum. He was expelled from Butt's Hill Middle School for trying to sell cigarettes to a dinner lady and then dumping her in the kitchen wheelie bin when she threatened to report him.

This brings me to my third clue.

CLUE 3

We were told this trip was an End-of-Spring-Term Reward for well-behaved students ... but Smokin' Joe is here.

If Smokin' Joe is a well-behaved student, then I'm a prize-winning turnip. There's trouble brewing, as Vigil-Aunty is always saying (as if trouble's something you drink with milk and sugar).

I try to warn Holly, Porter and the rest of the LOSERS, but no one listens until the 'Making the Modern World' gallery erupts in an explosion of smoke and engine noise.

"It's *alive!*" Holly grabs my head and angles it so we're both looking in the same direction. "That train thing is *alive!*"

"That 'train thing' is Stephenson's Rocket," I tell her. "Chosen as the best steam engine to power the railway in 1829."

"Seriously? You're geeking out on me *now*?" Holly grits her teeth. "Fine. Let me rephrase. That Stephenson's Rocket thing is *alive!*"

"Don't be silly, Holly. It's just an exhib— oooh . . ." My voice trails off as Stephenson's Rocket gives an impressive toot and releases a puff of smoke.

"Run for your lives before it flattens us all!" Holly squares her hips to face the engine, ready to save everyone, single-handedly.

"At ease, Wonder Woman," I say. "There are no tracks. Without them, Stephenson's Rocket is going nowhere. Even with tracks, its top speed was under thirty miles per hour, so all we'd have to do is step out of the way and let it power into the lift shaft."

"Jeez!" Porter slams his hands over his ears as a deep roar shakes the Science Museum. "What is that *noise*?"

"That would be the sound of the Apollo 10 command module's thrusters firing up," I yell over the racket as visitors run from all corners of the museum to see what's causing the commotion. "But that makes no sense. I doubt very much that the module has working thrusters, but *if* it did, and *if* they were firing, this place would be like a furnace." I look around the room. "And why is there *smoke* coming out of Stephenson's Rocket? It should be steam."

I move closer and spot the smoke bomb on the seat.

Thomas Edison! Trickery!

Now I know what I'm looking for, it takes me less than a minute to find smoke bombs and mini-speakers under all the major displays.

CLUE 4
Someone is deliberately making
it look like the museum exhibits
are coming to life.

"Red herring!" I yell. "None of this is real. It's just a distraction. Something bad is about to happen. Run away! Run away while you still have legs!"

I get a few odd looks, but no one runs – unless you count Smokin' Joe, who doesn't so much 'run away' as 'run towards', knocking into exhibits, setting off motion sensor alarms, smashing glass cases and turning 'Exploring Space' into a frenzy of howling security alarms, rioting children and people yelling wildly that everyone should "just calm down". One woman is so scared she's covered herself with a fire blanket, like a fancy-dress ghost but without the eye-holes.

"Good Lord!" A shrill voice cuts through the chaos. "What's happened to the Moon Rock?"

All heads swivel to the 'Exploring Space' gallery's prize exhibit.

The case is smashed and ...

CLUE 5
The Moon Rock is missing.

The security alarms continue to howl, but the volume in the room drops dramatically with a mass sucking-in of breath.

"Sit down!" an official voice commands. "Sit down exactly where you're standing. Nobody move."

I lower myself to the floor and stare at the empty glass case as Neanderthug Number One's voice thunders through my memory: "YOU GET MOON."

Looks like someone else wants the moon too.

Or is there a connection?

Hell Raizah doesn't seem like a museum kind of guy, but you never know. Plus, even if he had nothing to do with the disappearance, maybe this is an opportunity to save Dad. I'd never have stolen the rock myself. Obviously! I'm not a criminal. But what if I find it? Would it be okay to give it to Hell Raizah in exchange for Dad's safety? Maybe the museum would let me borrow it for a while as a thank you for locating it.

I study my fellow Science Museum visitors. Is the key to Dad's protection hidden in someone's pocket or handbag?

My eye twitches as another thought hits me. What if Dad's behind this? Is he trying to make his own deal with Hell Raizah? It's possible. Sometimes Dad can be too clever for his own good. He's a genius, but he forgets what's right and what's wrong when he's focusing on an invention or science experiment.

"Nobody move!" the official voice repeats as a woman scrambles to her feet, muttering about needing the toilet.

The official voice belongs to a small, bearded man wearing a badge that labels him 'Museum Curator'. He looks spookily similar to Vigil-Aunty's garden gnome, even down to the green trousers and waistcoat. All that's missing is the pointy hat.

Gnome?

Museum Curator Gnome paces up and down the 'Exploring Space' gallery, keeping time with the howling alarms, muttering under his breath and glaring at the empty display case. He's obviously important, because no one tells *him* to sit down.

"Good people of the Science Museum, we must find this Moon Rock with speed," he declares, tugging at his collar and sweating visibly. "The rock must be returned to its nitrogen-filled glass container and stored at a fixed temperature. It is perfectly safe under those conditions. But in the oxygen and humidity of the Earth's atmosphere ..." Museum Curator Gnome trails off as the security alarms fall silent.

Everyone stares at him expectantly.

"What?" Holly asks. "In the oxygen and humidity of the Earth's atmosphere – what?"

"If not stored correctly, certain unidentified properties within this particular Moon Rock could become dangerous to mankind. I fear, my dear child, we have an international incident on our hands."

That doesn't sound good. No one likes an international incident.

People start firing questions at Museum Curator Gnome:

"Dangerous – how?"

"What do these properties do?"

"COULD IT KILL US?" a voice shouts from the back.

We all look to Museum Curator Gnome, waiting for him to laugh and say, "Ha, don't be silly."

But he doesn't.

"How long have we got?" I ask.

Everyone laughs nervously, except the gnome. "Two weeks," he says. "I estimate we have two weeks before the first people's brains start to blow up. After that it will spread further and further."

"Blow up? Do you mean swell or actually explode? Hello? Hello?"

The Museum Curator Gnome signals that he won't be answering any more questions and walks across to join the other museum employees. The room shrinks under the weight of panic. You can learn a lot about people from how they handle life-threatening news.

Holly throws her biro at a space probe.

Porter misquotes an old Flash Gordon movie: "Flash, I love you ... but we only have fourteen days to save the Earth."

3

Lunar-cy

"He can't mean people's brains will literally explode, can he?" I ask, as we sit in the 'Exploring Space' gallery, staring at the empty Moon Rock case and waiting for the police to arrive.

"I think that's exactly what he means," Porter says. "If you measure panic in sweat patches, the Museum Curator guy's stress levels are off the scale."

Porter and Holly might not have IQs of one hundred and fifty-seven but they're smart in other ways. Porter often spots things I miss, like sweaty Museum Curator Gnomes, and he's brilliant at picking locks and making things work. Holly is good at, um, kicking things. Oh, and yelling at people until they tell us what we need to know. We make a good team.

"But what about the other missing Moon Rocks?" Holly interrupts my thoughts. "Remember that documentary we saw, Know-All? Tell Porter about the Irish Moon Rock."

It's hard to remember a time when we watched TV *without* Porter. We've done everything together since Mum invited him to live with us. It made sense. Porter had nowhere to stay – not only was his Mum on the run but his old dorm room had also been burned to the ground. And with Dad locked up, there was space in our house. Plus, having each other for company stopped us thinking too much about our notably absent criminal parents.

Since then, Porter, Holly and I have become a unit. Actually, not a 'unit' – that makes us sound efficient and coordinated. We're more of a three-headed beast with a multiple personality disorder.

"Hello?" snaps Holly, our impatient, prone-to-violence head. "Tell him the Irish Moon Rock story."

I try to remember the details. "After the Americans ended the Apollo moon missions, they shared their collection of Moon Rocks with countries around the world. Ireland was one of those countries and they kept their Apollo 11 Moon Rock in the Dunsink Observatory, until one morning in 1977. A fire started in the observatory, so they shifted all the debris from the fire to a landfill site across the street and didn't realise until too late that the Moon Rock was amongst the rubble."

"No!" Porter's eyes grow bigger. "They tipped the moon into a landfill site?!"

"Yup. The papers call it 'the pot of gold under a dump'. They reckon it's worth millions to anyone who finds it."

"Where was this landfill site?" Ms Meeks, the 'responsible adult' of our trip, shuffles across from her position with the other LOSERS, a few metres away. Nosy.

"Opposite Dunsink Observatory in Dublin,"

Holly tells her. "Why? Planning a holiday in Ireland, Miss?"

"Anyway," I say, with a loud cough. "The Irish rock has been missing since 1977 and the people there haven't gone mad or exploded or anything."

"I dunno," Porter says. "I've got an uncle from Ireland and he's completely bonkers ..."

"QUIET!" yells the Museum Curator Gnome. "The ladies and gentlemen of the Metropolitan Police have arrived and will be wishing to speak with you all. The return of the Moon Rock is of the utmost importance. I repeat, the utmost importance."

The police officers stride through the gallery, glaring at us in that forbidding police-person way that says, "Own up now – or else!"

Unfortunately, no one owns up. The police need to work on the 'or else' bit of their glare.

Two officers – one male and one female – conduct a thorough search of our bags and belongings. Visitors in the other parts of the Science Museum are allowed to leave, as long as they provide a contact address. But the police ask all of us in 'Exploring Space' to fill in a witness statement before we go.

An aggressive-looking policeman marches us to the museum's ground floor café and tells us to sit at one of the long tables and write up our reports. Aggressive Policeman patrols the room, pausing every few seconds to scowl at someone before moving on.

I glance around the table, from Remarkable Student Alexander to Remarkable Student Shazia, from Remarkable Student Giles to Remarkable Student Omar, from Porter to Holly, to Smokin' Joe ... urgh ... and then quickly away again.

I survey RS Alexander's clothes for Moon-Rock-shaped bulges. I've never trusted him.

"What if it was one of us?" I ask.

Aggressive Policeman's head snaps up as if I've confessed to murdering my own grandmother, which would be impressive as all four of my grandparents died before I was born.

"I'm not saying it was," I add quickly. "But it is possible, right?"

Everyone shushes me. Holly crushes my hand until the bones click. Aggressive Policeman makes his way round the table until he's standing opposite me. He reads my name from the top of my witness statement, pronouncing it as though it's an insult: "Noelle Hawkins."

Holly describes me as police-Marmite. It seems that every police officer I meet (and I've met a few now) either loves me or hates me. Sadly, despite my law-abiding nature, the haters outnumber the lovers.

In fact, as far as I can tell, PC Eric is the only police officer who loves me. (In a non-weird, fatherly kind of way.) And he's coming up for retirement.

"You can leave the crime-solving to us, *Noelle Hawkins*," Aggressive Policeman says. "Your role is to fill in that witness statement."

"It would help if we knew how the crime was committed." I pull out my notebook.

"Why don't you tell me, if you know so much?" Aggressive Policeman whips out a bigger notebook.

"Am I a suspect?" I quite like the idea. "Are we all suspects?"

I study my fellow LOSERS. You couldn't find a less-likely looking bunch of criminals if you tried. Type 'teen nerds' into Google images and you'll probably find a picture of Shazia, Omar and Giles. You might have to type 'posh teen nerd' to get Remarkable Student Alexander. Who knows what you'd have to type to get an image of Smokin' Joe? 'Primeval troglodyte' might do it. The trickle of blood from his nose could be the result of a run-in with a woolly mammoth.

As I glance at the blood, I get a prickling sensation at the back of my neck. This isn't Smokin' Joe's first nosebleed today and I've learned to be suspicious of nosebleeds. I get out my notepad.

CLUE 6

Smokin' Joe (who I have never seen
have a nosebleed) has
started having nosebleeds.

"Suspects?" Aggressive Policeman's sneer shatters my thoughts. "This was a professional job, not something a bunch of silly school kids could have pulled off. I'm simply following procedure. You were close to the exhibit at the time of the theft. You might have seen something important without realising."

We might not look like master criminals, but it's wrong to write us off as 'silly school kids'. Except for Smokin' Joe. It's probably best to write him off. That boy has the brain capacity of a garden slug.

"Can I see your clues?" I ask.

"No, Miss flaming Marple, you can't," Aggressive Policeman snaps. "This is an important police investigation, not a game of Cluedo. Just write down what happened while you were in the museum."

"Shouldn't you interview each of us separately, to see if our stories corroborate?" I ask.

Aggressive Policeman balls his hands into fists.

Previous experience with angry officers of the law

suggests this would be a good time for me to stop talking.

Jabbing his finger at my paper, Aggressive Policeman says, "Just write a factual account of what happened during your trip. And do it without speaking."

4

My Trip Record

11:10	The eight members of our school trip and Ms Meeks get on the school minibus. (see Diagram A - Bus)
11:11	Ms Meeks asks Smokin' Joe to remove his headphones. He doesn't.
11:12	Smokin' Joe says he feels travel sick. I point out that the bus hasn't moved yet.
11:13	RS Shazia screams that Smokin' Joe is picking his nose and wiping it on her.
11:14	Ms Meeks tells Smokin' Joe to stop picking his nose. He doesn't. Ms Meeks tells RS Shazia to stop screaming. She doesn't.
11:16	Minibus Driver charges down the bus, throws a sick bag and a loo roll at Smokin' Joe's head and drags RS Shazia to the snot-free seat beside me (see Diagram A - Bus), telling her to "Shut up or get off the bus."
11:18	RS Shazia stops screaming long enough to threaten to report Minibus Driver for unnecessary use of force.

	Minibus Driver points out that RS Shazia can only report him if he doesn't chop her up and hide the pieces in motorway service stations across the UK first.
	RS Shazia agrees there's nothing to report.
11:20	Ms Meeks asks RS Alexander if he wants to move away from Smokin' Joe too.
	RS Alexander says he'll stay where he is and "look after poor Joe."
11:21	I tug my ears to check they're working. Did RS Alexander just offer to help someone?

Diagram A - Bus

Aggressive Policeman rests one hand on the café table and peers over my shoulder. "Your bus journey is irrelevant," he says. "Start at the Science Museum."

"With all due respect," I say, "when you've worked on more cases, you'll realise it's impossible to tell what is and isn't relevant until the case is solved."

Aggressive Policeman pokes *Diagram A – Bus*, pushing so hard his knuckle goes white. "With all due respect," he says, mimicking my voice, "I'm not surprised the seats near you on the bus were empty."

RS Alexander sniggers.

"Start. At. The. Science. Museum," Aggressive Policeman repeats. "Or. I. Confiscate. Your. Pen."

"Police brutality," I mutter and consider drawing Aggressive Policeman beneath the wheels of *Diagram A – Bus*.

Instead, I continue my record of our trip – from the minute we arrived at the museum.

2:08	Minibus Driver gives us two minutes to get off the bus before he takes advantage of being able to take his hands off the steering wheel and uses them to throttle us.
2:09	The minibus is empty.
2:10	Ms Meeks splits us into pairs – putting me with Smokin' Joe. I explain that Holly, Porter and I are a trio. Ms Meeks explains that if I don't want to be paired up with Smokin' Joe, she'll pair me with the Minibus Driver. I shuffle closer to Smokin' Joe, ready to defend myself. Joe just nods at me and continues listening to his iPod. Maybe he really is sick.
2:18	The museum tour begins.
2:19	RS Alexander goes to the bathroom.

2:40	RS Alexander remains in the bathroom. Porter joins him.
2:50	RS Alexander is STILL in the bathroom. I ask the security guards to check whether he's fallen down the loo. They ignore me and listen to their turquoise walkie-talkies.
2:51	Both Porter and RS Alexander reappear. (No thanks to walkie-talkie guards.)
2:55	RS Alexander flinches at every sound as if he's expecting something big to happen.
2:57	Smokin' Joe's nose starts bleeding and blood spurts on to the Mars Lander. The museum guide asks when we're leaving.
3:00	BOOM! The gallery shakes with the sound of engines firing up. Everyone squeals that the exhibits are coming to life. (Everyone watches too much TV). I explain the chaos is the result of smoke bombs and sound f/x. No one listens.
3:01	Smokin' Joe runs around, smashing glass and setting off alarms. Ms Meeks tells Smokin' Joe to stand still. He doesn't. Mass panic, including a woman under a fire blanket who keeps knocking into things.
3:07	A museum official announces the Moon Rock is missing and orders us to sit down. More alarms go off.
3:30	The police arrive . . .

Aggressive Policeman collects the records and asks us to remain in our seats. No one else's report fills two sides of the A4 paper. The police must be glad I'm here.

It's the details that count.

5

Majority Rules

The museum café serves light lunches and a range of daily specials like pizza, pasta bakes and soup. I know this because it says so on their menu board. Also, I can smell them. However, the museum café is not serving those things to me, because I have no money and because the serving staff are waiting to be questioned. It's been hours since lunch and by the time Aggressive Policeman marches back in I've started to wonder which of my fellow LOSERS I'd eat first.

"Right, LOSERS." Aggressive Policeman slams the reports on the table. "We need to iron out a few discrepancies between your statements."

Smokin' Joe screws up his face. "You want us to iron?"

"It's a metaphor," I tell him, wrinkling my nose as I smell something burning. I wonder if that happens a lot. (The burning I mean. I don't wrinkle my nose any more than the average person.) I've never seen a place with as much firefighting equipment as this museum café – extinguishers, sand buckets, fire blankets and the works. I don't know whether it makes me feel safer or more alarmed.

"I ain't ironing no metaphor," Smokin' Joe mutters. "My dad says ironing is girls' work."

"I'm a girl and I don't iron," Holly says. "Porter usually does it before I get the chance." She ignores Porter's squeak of protest and pokes Joe in the chest. "So, your dad is talking absolute—"

"When you've finished, geniuses," Aggressive Policeman interrupts, "there's some confusion about the length of time Alexander West was missing from the group."

"No time at all," Remarkable Student Alexander protests. "Unless you count a quick toilet break."

"Quick? You were gone for over thirty minutes," I say.

"More like five." Alexander stares at Shazia, Omar and Giles until they murmur in agreement.

"We'll go with the majority," Aggressive Policeman says, scribbling in his notebook.

"Why?" I protest. "Why go with the majority when the majority is wrong? Go with the person who's right – me!" I add, in case that part's not clear.

Porter pulls my sleeve and murmurs under his breath, "He wasn't in the toilet."

"Huh?"

"I don't know where Alexander was," Porter whispers, "but he wasn't in the toilet."

I try to share this important clue with Aggressive Policeman.

CLUE 7
Remarkable Student Alexander
lied about where he went.
And Shazia, Omar and Giles
lied to cover up his lies.

Aggressive Policeman isn't interested. "What about Joe Slater? Was he, or was he not, close to the Moon Rock when it vanished?"

I'd be more than happy for them to lock up Smokin' Joe and throw away the key, so it's hard to admit, "He was nowhere near it."

"That's not what your friends think." Aggressive Policeman scowls.

"I saw Joe smash the glass," Holly says apologetically.

I nod. "But he was on the other side of the room when the Moon Rock disappeared."

"How can you be sure?" Aggressive Policeman glances at the wall clock, clearly keen to move things along.

"Because I can picture it." I close my eyes and visualise my last glimpse of the Moon Rock, less than a minute before Museum Curator Gnome announced its disappearance. Smokin' Joe is at least ten metres away from the smashed display case.

"What do you mean, 'picture it'?" Aggressive Policeman snaps.

"Know-All has a photographic memory," Holly says. "She can remember everything she sees."

"Then she must have had her eyes closed," Remarkable Student Shazia says. "Because Joe

Slater was right next to that Moon Rock. I saw him."

Alexander, Giles and Omar nod in agreement.

CLUE 8

The Remarkable Students are claiming to have seen things they couldn't have seen.

"Great," I mutter. "Another majority. I guess that means he must have been where they say he was."

Aggressive Policeman seems to think so. He notes it in his book and clicks the end of his pen, up and down, up and down, staring at me.

"What?" I ask.

"Why does your account differ from everyone else's?"

"Because everyone else is wrong?"

"Are you saying your friends are lying?" Aggressive Policeman asks.

"No. I'm saying the Remarkable Students are lying and my *friends* weren't paying enough attention."

"Guilty as charged," Holly admits.

"Someone else must have seen what I saw," I say. "What about the woman under the blanket?"

"What woman under the blanket?" Aggressive Policeman flicks through his reports.

Remarkable Student Alexander points at me and then twirls his fingers beside his head, making the universal sign for 'crazy person'.

Aggressive Policeman's mouth tightens. "You do not want to play games with me, young lady."

"Absolutely not," I agree. No way would I ever sit down to a game of Cluedo with Aggressive Policeman. He strikes me as a very bad loser.

Aggressive Policeman scribbles something else in his notebook.

"What are you writing?" I ask. "What have I done?"

"Why don't *you* tell *me*?" This seems to be Aggressive Policeman's idea of sharp interrogation.

"How can I tell you if I don't know?"

"What *do* you know?"

"Lots of things. My sister's right, I have a photographic memory. I can remember everything I've—"

Aggressive Policeman raises his hand. "Not interested in your memory," he says, "Tell me what you know about the Moon Rock."

"I wrote everything in my statement. If you read it properly, instead of ignoring it because it doesn't match everyone else's, you'll see—"

"Watch your attitude," Aggressive Policeman blusters. "You think you're smarter than the police because you've got some kind of photogenic memory...?

"Photographic," I point out politely. "I doubt my memory looks particularly good in pictures."

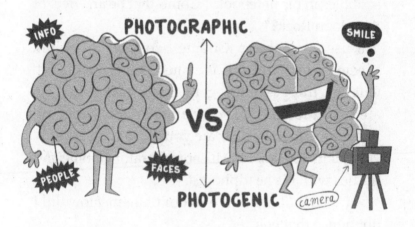

PHOTOGRAPHIC

INFO

SMILE

VS

PEOPLE

FACES

PHOTOGENIC   camera

"Photographic, photogenic, photic-schmotic. I don't care, Miss. Let me tell you—"

I don't get to hear what he's planning to tell me because we're interrupted by the Museum Curator Gnome.

"Which of you young folk would be Noelle and Holly Hawkins?" He glances from our table to the other school party.

I'm about to step forward when I notice his shirt sleeves are covered in blood.

He sees me flinch. "Fear not, small person. This blood is not mine. It came from the nasal passages of one of our poor, unfortunate security guards."

Reassuring. Not.

"Nosebleed, you say?" Aggressive Policeman scribbles in his notebook. "Could that be an effect of the Moon Rock?"

Museum Curator Gnome scratches his chin. "Seems a bit early, but we must be on our guard. One of these young gentlemen was similarly affected, I recall." He spots Smokin' Joe. "You, my fine young fellow! How are your nasal passages?"

Smokin' Joe ignores Museum Curator Gnome and fiddles with his headphones.

Archimedes! Look at the colour of them. How did I not notice that before?

CLUE 9
Smokin' Joe is wearing
turquoise headphones.

"Excuse me." I pull the gnome's sleeve, carefully avoiding the blood. "Did the security guard with the nosebleed have a turquoise walkie-talkie?"

"What a strange question, child. I have more important things to do than … Wait! Yes, I think he did. I noticed something off about the fellow, but I was too busy being bled on to give it my full attention. Turquoise walkie-talkies? Yes, indeed. Whatever next?"

I look at Holly and Porter. They're already looking at me. So is Museum Curator Gnome.

He peers over his glasses at my face. "You're one of the Hawkins girls, aren't you? Striking family resemblance." He turns to peer at Holly. "You too. A less striking resemblance, but it's still there. The daughters of Professor 'Big Brain' Brian, I presume?"

I nod. Aggressive Policeman's lips twist and he makes another note in his book. I try not to sink in my chair. I used to be proud when people linked me to Dad, but that was when he was just a famous celebrity scientist. Now he's an infamous crazy-scientist who faked his own death by blowing up a public toilet.

Museum Curator Gnome doesn't seem to hold that against him. "Terribly sorry to hear of your father's misfortunes," he says. "He was a wonderful supporter of the Science Museum and a splendidly clever fellow. He'd have found a solution to this dreadful situation. When I discovered his daughters were on the premises I thought you might be able to help – I didn't realise how small you'd be. Still, I'm sure you'll be smashingly bright when you're older, just like your father. I was devastated when I heard he'd perished. Delighted to discover he'd just … er … just …"

"Just blown up a public toilet and pretended to be dead?" Holly spits out the words in disgust.

"Mmm. Yes. That." Museum Curator Gnome nods.

"I'm not that young," I point out. "I'm twelve and I have an IQ of one hundred and fifty-seven."

Museum Curator Gnome isn't listening. "Do ask the old chap if he plans to return and complete his research after his … break. Shouldn't be embarrassed about … er … you know. These things happen to us all."

I'm so busy wondering what Museum Curator Gnome gets up to in his spare time if he thinks being arrested for exploding a toilet 'happens to us all' that I forget to ask what Dad was researching.

Never mind. I know who can tell me about the research. And the nosebleeds. And the moon connection.

Dad.

Luckily I've already booked a visit for tomorrow.

6

Softer Cell

Days Left to Save the Earth: 13

I stride through the Prison Visitors' Centre. Vigil-Aunty scuttles along behind me. The metal detector doesn't scare me now I've swapped to multivitamins-with-zinc, which have the added benefit of protecting me from jail germs.

Dad joins us at Table Eight, looking much better than he did last time. Maybe he's taking zinc too. His limp is gone, the bruises are fading and his nose is more Ernie from *Sesame Street* than Rudolph the Red-Nosed Reindeer. Plus he's shaved off the stupid goatee beard he grew when he was the Great Leader of LOSERS.

It's harder to be mad at him when he looks like the Dad I remember.

"How are the Neanderthugs?" I ask.

The smile wobbles and Dad glances over his shoulder, relaxing when he sees no one's listening. "All good."

"So tell me what happened at the Science Museum," I whisper.

"I don't know what you mean."

"Of course you do ... *Louis Pasteur!*" I cling to my chair as Hell Raizah approaches. "How can one man be so *big*?"

Vigil-Aunty reaches for her Handbag of Mass Destruction, forgetting she had to leave it with security. I doubt it would have worked against Hell Raizah anyway. He's built to withstand Armageddon. Like a large cockroach. With biceps.

He slaps Dad on the back in a way you'd only welcome if you had mints blocking your windpipe. But there are signs it might have been intended as a friendly whack as Hell Raizah is carrying a fluffy moon toy with miniature arms and legs and he lifts one of the spindly arms to give Dad a wave.

Freaky. Yet interesting.

CLUE 10
Hell Raizah wants the moon
(because, weirdly, he's convinced it will
make him stronger) and a piece of the
moon has been stolen.

CLUE 11
The Neanderthugs are being
abnormally friendly to Dad.

"Why so chummy?" I narrow my eyes at Dad as Hell Raizah gives him another moon-man wave and the Neanderthug at Table Two gives a cheery thumbs-up. "They're treating you like ..." I pause for a millisecond.

Vigil-Aunty leaps in to fill the gap. "Like the winner of a criminal *X-Factor* competition."

Dad rolls his eyes "Wasn't 'Introduce Similes Into Your Life Week' last week, Vera?"

"It was." Vigil-Aunty nods. "But I'm struggling with 'Embrace Onomatopoeia Week'."

"BANG!" Dad slams his hand on the table.

"For goodness' sake, Brian," Vigil-Aunty protests as the guards look over.

"Just demonstrating onomatopoeia," Dad says. "WHAM!" he slaps his hand down again.

I giggle at the expression on Vigil-Aunty's face, but I know Dad's trying to change the subject and I won't let him.

"So, Dad, *why* are they being so nice to you?"

Dad shrugs. "Probably because I've been teaching them a bit of English."

"But they *are* English," I remind him.

"Not so you'd notice," Dad mutters. "I may have taught them a bit of ICT too."

"ICT? What are you talking about?" Vigil-Aunty nostrils flare. "You are not allowed access to a computer or any other technology in here, Brian. The judge said so."

Dad gives me a wink. I have no idea why.

Probably best that way. I don't want to become an accessory (as in 'a person who assists with crime' not 'a human hair scrunchie'). Plus, I have other, more important, things to find out.

"Why didn't you tell me about your research at the Science Museum?" I ask.

"Never came up," Dad mumbles.

"Research? What research?" Vigil-Aunty screeches. "This better not have anything to do with those brain rays, Brian. Not after they caused all that trouble last time."

"All three brain rays were destroyed," I begin ... and then I remember Smokin' Joe's nosebleed. "At least that's what Dad told me. Right, Dad?"

Dad does more mumbling. "One melted in the fire and another was disabled by a top-secret government organisation called the **B**ureau **A**gainst **D**angerous **D**evices in Ireland, England and Scotland."

"What about Wales?" Vigil-Aunty asks.

"Wales must have opted out."

"More importantly, what about the other brain ray?" I ask. "It wasn't destroyed, was it, Dad? Don't lie. I'll know and I'll hate it."

Dad stares at his hands and says, barely loud enough to hear, "It's in a safe place."

I don't believe it. As if the Moon Rock wasn't enough to worry about.

"Tell me where it is." I glance at the clock. "And tell me what you've done with the Moon Rock. We don't have much time. The world needs saving. You need to start talking."

"How do I know I can trust you?" Dad asks. "You haven't been very good at keeping my secrets so far."

I gasp. How unfair is that?

It's Vigil-Aunty's turn to slam her fist on Table Eight.

"CRASH!" Dad shouts.

"Oh, shut up, Brian!" Vigil-Aunty snaps. "Noelle's the only member of your family who can stand to be near you, and now you're upsetting her too. Frying children's brains is not a 'secret', you stupid man – it's a crime. Where is your remorse? Where are the apologies? You haven't even asked how my sister is. And what about Holly?"

Dad rocks back on his chair, looking ashamed but grumpy. He doesn't like being told off. He likes being told how great he is ... Aha! That might work.

48

"The policeman told us the Moon Rock theft was a professional job." I watch Dad's face. "The work of a criminal mastermind."

Vigil-Aunty mutters something about 'criminal mastermind' being an oxymoron. Dad looks tempted to onomatopoeia-ify her again.

"Was it you, Dad?" I ask. "Were you the criminal mastermind?"

"How could I be when I was locked in here?"

"That's what I want to know. I know you were involved, Dad. How did you do it? Does this have something to do with these ICT lessons?"

Dad smiles. Even when he's trying to keep things secret he likes it when I figure things out. But all he says is, "So many questions, Know-All."

"And so few answers," I reply. "Can you at least tell me about the research you were doing?"

Dad chews his fingernails.

"Or tell me why Hell Raizah's so happy."

More fingernail nibbling.

I jump to my feet and then quickly sit back down again when scary criminals turn to stare at me. "I need to know what's going on, Dad. Removing the Moon Rock from its case put everyone's life in danger. I'm going to be busy saving the world, so if you won't help me by telling me what you know, I won't have time to visit you for a while."

Dad slumps in his chair, his shoulders drooping, but I refuse to feel sorry for him.

"I mean it, Dad. If you won't speak to me then I don't see the point in coming back."

"What if I give you a clue?"

"What kind of clue?"

Dad doesn't answer. The prison guards announce visiting time is almost over.

I pinch my lips together and tap my fingers on the table. I hate the woolliness of the word 'clue' but I need to find out what Dad knows. Growling in frustration, I mutter, "Okay, I'll come back if you give me a clue."

Dad edges his chair closer and whispers, "Ask your friend Porter about the museum volunteers."

7

Any Volunteers?

Porter is squatting in the oak tree outside Holly's bedroom window when we get home. It's Vigil-Aunty's fault he's happier outside, balancing on a branch, than in here with us. Even though Mum clearly invited Porter to stay for as long as he wants while his mother's missing, Vigil-Aunty keeps asking what his plans are and telling everyone who'll listen that Mum should never have taken him in.

I've told Porter not to take it personally – if everyone Vigil-Aunty has offended this month sat in our tree, there'd be no room left on the branch for him. But he still won't come inside, which is annoying because it's hard to hold a conversation through a window.

"What did Dad mean about the volunteers?"

"No idea." Porter doesn't look up, just sits there shredding leaves.

"Please come in," I say. "I feel ill watching you perch out there like some sort of over-sized squirrel."

"Nice simile. Vigil-Aunty would be proud." Holly leans out of the window to yell at Porter. "Stop being an idiot. Come in and tell us what you know."

"I don't know anything. And I'm not coming in. I like it out here. Fresh air helps me think."

"Then start thinking about what Dad meant," Holly snaps.

"I already told you. I. Don't. Know."

"Liar." Holly throws a hairbrush at him. "Fine. You sit out there looking for nuts while Know-All and I solve this case on our own." She makes a big thing of pulling the window down, but I notice she leaves it open a crack at the bottom.

"Looks like it's down to us, Know-All," she says with her bossy face on. "We need a list of museum volunteers and a lift to the Science Museum. You get the list and I'll pester Uncle Max for the lift. It shouldn't be hard to convince him. Vigil-Aunty will like the idea. She's always saying that you need to get out more and that I should do some educational activities."

The window creaks upwards. Porter's head

appears through the gap, like an eighteenth-century French royal awaiting the guillotine.

"No need to ask what your aunt says about me." He tries to laugh but his eyebrows look sad. "On the positive side, she won't want to leave me here 'weaselling my way' into your mum's affections, so she should be happy for me to tag along."

I pat his hand awkwardly.

Holly reaches for his other hand and uses it to yank him further into the room. "It would be much easier if you'd just tell us what you know."

"I'm sure it would," Porter says. "If I actually knew anything."

Holly mutters something about fetching her chainsaw to torture to the truth out of him, but, for once, she decides to let it go.

Next morning, the three of us pile into the back of Uncle Max's Ford Focus and set off for the Science Museum.

Uncle Max yells out of the car window as we push our way through the pack of reporters at the museum entrance. "You've got two hours to do whatever it is you kids have to do."

Things start well when we bump into Museum Curator Gnome wandering through 'Exploring Space'.

"Miniature Hawkins people ... and friend!" His

cheery greeting clashes with his general air of gloom and slumpiness. "What a coincidence. I was looking at your father's research this morning. Such a clever man. How the devil is he?"

"He's fine," I say and then yelp as Holly prods me. "You say you were looking at his research? We'd love to hear more about it."

"I shall go one better and show you." Museum Curator Gnome shuffles off, gesturing for us to follow. "It gladdens my miserable heart to see friendly faces."

Odd thing to say. I wonder who the *un*friendly faces belong to. We stop in front of a big red plastic wall. Written on the wall it says:

LIVE SCIENCE

Welcome to Live Science. Here visitors take part in real scientific experiments to find out more about themselves.

Nothing dangerous ... just fun, interesting experiments – such as when scientists discovered how playing video games affects people's mood and immune systems, or when visitors helped scientists find out that some people see colours and shapes when they hear sounds.

This is science in action, so come and join us for the next Live Science and find out more about who you are.

"This is our Live Science lab," the gnome explains. "It gives scientists like your father a chance to conduct research on some of the two and a half million visitors we get each year."

"What was Dad researching?" I ask. "Brain stuff, I suppose?"

Museum Curator Gnome shakes his head. "No. He was exploring what it means to 'see' things." He shows us Dad's entry in the laboratory log book.

CLUE 13

Dad was exploring how the camera lens
sees things differently from the human eye.

Museum Curator Gnome jumps when his mobile rings. He scrabbles for it and slaps it to his ear. "I have to take this," he tells us, a muscle jerking in his cheek. "They want me to talk to the press about the Moon Rock investigation. We're under pressure. Time is running out."

"Time's running out for us too." Holly glances at her watch as the gnome strides away. "Uncle Max will be back before we know it. Where next?"

"Dad's research has to be a clue," I say.

Porter nods. "Maybe it's something to do with the security cameras? Your dad and my mother had an entire CCTV Room in the LOSERS building before the science teacher blew it up."

"Brilliant, Porter!" I give him a thumbs-up.

CLUE 14

Dad and Ms Grimm were obsessed
with security cameras in the
Case of the Exploding Loo.

"We need to find out if there's anything unusual about the camera footage from the time the Moon Rock went missing."

"Let's split up," Holly suggests. "Make the most of the time we've got left. See what you can find out about the cameras and meet back in 'Exploring Space' in half an hour. Porter, this would also be a good time to remember anything you know about the museum volunteers."

8

Watt's Up?

Days Left to Save the Earth: 12

As Porter and Holly race off in different directions, I go in search of Museum Curator Gnome. I want to ask him what makes this Moon Rock so dangerous. How can the Irish Moon Rock be missing for so long with no ill-effects if this one is set to trigger some kind of international exploding head Armageddon?

I find Museum Curator Gnome in the 'James Watt and Our World' gallery, talking to a white plaster head.

He looks up as I approach. "Hello again, young lady. May I introduce you to my silent friend?" He pats the case containing the plaster sculpture.

"Right. Um, hello, Mr Watt," I greet the fake head.

"You're already acquainted?"

"I've read about him." I close my eyes and picture the page. "He was an engineer and a hero of the Industrial Revolution. They named the 'watt' measurement after him to honour his contribution to science."

"A hero, eh?" Museum Curator Gnome nods sadly. "Honoured in his lifetime and remembered forever for his inventions and achievements. Lucky chap. I wonder how I'll be remembered – probably as the silly old fool who endangered the world by losing a piece of the moon."

"I'm sure that's not true," I say, wishing I was better at cheering people up. "Most people don't know much about James Watt, so they probably won't remember anything at all about you."

Museum Curator Gnome's heavy sigh suggests that's no consolation.

"Maybe the missing Moon Rock isn't as big a problem as you think it is," I try to reassure him. "Other Moon Rocks have gone missing without harming anybody."

Museum Curator Gnome glances around the room and then moves his mouth closer to my ear and whispers, "This Moon Rock is different."

"How?" I whisper back.

"Different properties," he murmurs. "Unidentified. Not entirely lunar."

Huh? "How can a Moon Rock be 'not entirely lunar'?"

"The chaps at NASA suspect it came from a meteorite that collided with the moon."

CLUE 15
The Moon Rock is not necessarily
a *Moon* Rock.

Oooh. "So it's a 'Somewhere in Space Rock' rather than a Moon Rock?"

"Shh." Museum Curator Gnome checks behind us. "Not so loud."

"Could that be a reason for someone to steal it?"

"No. Because no one knew. Not even the fine brains at NASA until last month, when they started testing the other rock taken from this sector of Mare Nubium and experienced shocking results."

"Mare Nubium?" I flick through my memory:

Mare Nubium, translated as 'sea of clouds': a dark plain on the face of the moon nearest the Earth.

"What kind of shocking results?" I ask.

"The top-secret kind. Death, destruction, people going crazy and attacking each other. Brains exploding. That sort of thing."

"Literally exploding?" I ask. "How is that possible?"

"The NASA chaps said something about the rock's properties reacting with Earth's atmosphere to create a low-oxygen environment."

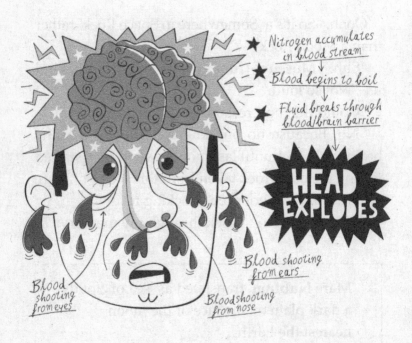

Nitrogen accumulates in blood stream

Blood begins to boil

Fluid breaks through blood/brain barrier

HEAD EXPLODES

Blood shooting from eyes

Blood shooting from nose

Blood shooting from ears

"Like altitude sickness?" I ask. "That can make your brain swell if fluid breaks through the blood-brain barrier."

"No one is entirely sure, to be honest, but it sounds squelchy, unpleasant and to be avoided at all costs. NASA were going to exchange our rock for a less explosive piece of the moon next week, under cover of darkness. But it's too late now."

"Why all the secrecy?"

"NASA didn't want to cause a panic. They made me swear not to tell a soul."

"You just told me," I point out.

Museum Curator Gnome waves his hand in a gesture that I suspect is supposed to mean 'I'm very important and I don't have to listen to NASA', but in reality makes him look like a short, bearded contestant in a beauty pageant. "The time has come to cause a panic. This information must be shared with my worthy colleagues and the ladies and gentlemen of the press." Museum Curator Gnome casts a nervous glance at the reporters swarming through the museum. "The rock must be found."

I remember Dad's research. "It might help us find it if you could tell me anything about the CCTV cameras on the day of the robbery."

"CCTV cameras?" Museum Curator Gnome gives me a vacant stare and turns back to James Watt.

"Wouldn't have a clue, young lady. You'll need to talk to security."

"I just wondered if anything unusual happened that day."

"Many unusual things happened that day." As Museum Curator Gnome's face sags, I notice his hair is unwashed and he's wearing the same clothes as last time I saw him. "They blame me, you know." He looks around furtively and then, in a dramatic whisper, says, *"I hear their thoughts."*

Uh-oh. It seems Museum Curator Gnome might be going a tiny bit insane. Is this the first sign of the exploding brain apocalypse?

I give him a weak smile and edge backwards until I reach the kindly-looking woman at the front desk. "Hello ... Miriam," I read from her name badge. "I think the Museum Gno— I mean Curator, needs help. He's ill. Paranoid. Says everyone blames him for what's happened."

Miriam screws up her kind face until she resembles an angry walnut. "Maybe he's right. He can't keep secrets from us any more. We all know what he's up to."

Archimedes! Beneath that gentle exterior, Miriam is a festering pit of fury. Is no one what they seem around here?

"I'll ... er ... talk to someone else, shall I?" I

mutter, scuttling off in the direction of two security guards.

They grimace when I mention the Museum Curator Gnome, who seems to have wandered off anyway, so I give up on him and ask to see the CCTV footage instead.

They laugh. "We don't share that kind of information with children."

I wonder if flattery only works on Dad or if it's good for all men of his age. Nothing to lose by trying. "You are clearly very conscientious security guards."

The taller guard keeps on laughing.

"Oi!" The other guard pokes him. "You think that's a joke? You don't agree that I'm a conscientious guard?"

Tall Security Guard stops laughing. "Don't be stupid."

"So now I'm stupid as well as useless?"

"I didn't say you were stupid. I told you not to *be* stupid."

"There you go again, trying to fool me with words. You think you're smarter than I am. Don't deny it."

"Don't be sill …" Tall Security Guard begins to defend himself but Other Security Guard stares at him until his cheeks go red. "Sorry," Tall Guard mutters.

Hmm. Something weird is going on here.

I glance at my watch. Time to meet the others –
and I've got nothing. Unless you count a feeling of
complete confusion.

Holly has been equally useless. She kicks the wall
in irritation. "They seemed to know what I wanted
to ask before I opened my mouth, and they had no
intention of answering. Still, at least we're where
we're supposed to be. Where's Porter?"

We find him in the gift shop, talking to the girl on
the till. Her hand is on his arm and she must have
something in her eye because she keeps fluttering
her eyelashes at him.

"She needs an eyebath," I tell Holly. "And a bottle
of water. Look how dehydrated she is. She keeps
licking her lips."

"She's not dehydrated, you donut. She's flirting
with Porter!"

"Seriously?" I stare at the girl in astonishment.
She must be at least two years older than him.

"Weird. Do you reckon she's the volunteer Dad was talking about?"

"No, idiot. Gift shop workers get paid." Holly hits the wall violently, making me jump.

"I was only asking," I protest. "No need to destroy the building."

"Whatever!" Holly says. "Anyway, that girl doesn't look smart enough to be part of any plan."

Whoa! Mean! Holly's not usually mean. What's put her in such a bad mood? I'm guessing Porter, from the way she's scowling at him as he heads towards us. Gift Shop Girl waves goodbye, tossing her hair over her shoulder.

No hair tossing for Holly. Instead, she kicks a shelf of NASA toy spacesuits and yells, "What do you think you're playing at, Porter? We've been knocking ourselves out hunting for clues and interviewing witnesses while you've been – what? Collecting girlfriends?"

Porter's ears turn red and he giggles. "Collecting girlfriends? I didn't know that's what I was doing. Cool!"

"Not cool." Holly glares at him.

Porter is no match for that stare. He looks down and tries to change the subject. "Okay, since you've been so efficient, why don't you tell me what you've learned?"

"That's not important," Holly lies, fiddling with a NASA space glove. "What's important is we've been trying. Unlike you."

"I've been conducting my own investigation."

"That's not what it looked like from here." Holly hits him with the space glove.

Porter snatches the glove and points a NASA finger at her. "Ha. Then how do I know that at the time of the Moon Rock's disappearance a security camera blacked out in the 'Investigating Alien Worlds' section?"

CLUE 17
One of the cameras wasn't functioning at
the time of the robbery.

I clap my hands together. "Good work, Porter!"

He bows. "I like to think so."

"We should stop calling it a Moon Rock though." I tell them what I learned from Museum Curator Gnome.

"Space Rock it is then." Holly turns to poke Porter. "So you were only being nice to that girl to get information?"

Porter's nod upsets me, although it seems to

make Holly happy. I don't like to imagine him being fake-nice. Vigil-Aunty's voice echoes through my head: *"All charm, that boy, weaselling his way into people's homes."*

Porter wiggles NASA glove fingers at me, making me feel disloyal for doubting him. I tune back in to what he's saying: "My new friend explained the camera didn't cover the Moon – sorry – *Space* Rock, so the police are treating it as a coincidence."

"I don't believe in coincidences," I say, my mind back on the case.

"Nor do I," Porter says. "The gift shop girl also said the police are convinced a schoolboy was involved. I don't think it's a coincidence that their description matches Smokin' Joe either."

9

Fear Of Frying Pans

Days Left to Save the Earth: 11

I tug at a loose bit of wool on the cuff of my jumper
as we sit on the wall outside Smokin' Joe's house,
waiting for him to come back from the shop so we
can interrogate him about his role in the Moon
Rock's disappearance.

Smokin' Joe as a suspect? For a bungled
smash-and-grab robbery, maybe. But as part of a
skilled criminal gang? Not so much. Something is
going on. Something connected with his nosebleeds.

CLUE 18
In the Science Museum, Smokin' Joe
displayed the symptoms people
experienced after being zapped by the
brain ray in the Case of the Exploding Loo.

There is no way the Smokin' Joe I know could have planned a Space Rock heist. But what if he's been increasing his brain power with the missing brain ray? Admittedly, there hasn't been much sign of superior intelligence from him, but I can't rule the idea out.

"Einstein!" I mutter as my cuff starts to unravel.

Holly grabs my wrist and bites off the end of the wool. "It's fine."

"It's not fine. Look at the massive hole."

"Just stick your thumb through it. You wanted fingerless gloves."

I glare at my sister. "Fingerless gloves, yes. Fingerless jumper, no. It makes me look neglected."

"Then you'll blend in perfectly," Porter says. "The Slaters' house is like a shrine to the God of Neglect."

"No such god," I say.

"Bet there is," Porter retorts. "Bet there's a Greek one. The Greeks had a god for everything."

"Aphro-forgot-to-tidy?" Holly giggles.

"Shh," I hiss. "No silliness during investigations."

But Porter's right about the state of the Slaters' house. The walls are crumbling, the window frames are cracked and the guttering is hanging down, dripping water on to the five square metres of weeds and old junk that make up the Slaters' front yard. A deformed tree grows in the middle of the concrete, pressing close to the house and adding to the gloom.

Through the broken front window, we can hear the buzz of daytime TV presenters discussing the threat from the Space Rock. An American reporter has revealed a cover-up at a NASA facility in the US, where a whole town was secretly quarantined last month after they took a Mare Nubium space rock sample out of its case for testing and it sent the local population into a frenzy.

I'd like to hear what they're saying, as the presenter is asking the American journalist whether he found any evidence of brains exploding, but their voices are drowned out by Ma Slater screaming down the phone at someone called 'You-Useless-Piece-of-Poo'. ('Poo' isn't the exact word she used.)

Smokin' Joe lurches into view at the end of the street, stuffing his face with crisps – turquoise earphones in his ears and a dazed expression on his face. At least there's no blood trickling from his nose today. He hasn't spotted us yet and lumbers down the road in our direction. When he reaches his front gate, he hacks up a ball of spit and gobs on the floor.

"You honestly think he's had his brain *boosted*?" Porter murmurs.

"He did start from a very low base," I say uncertainly.

"One way to find out." Holly leaps up from the wall and yells, "Hand over the brain ray, Joe Slater, or you'll regret it!"

It's a vague threat, but that doesn't matter. The sudden movement is enough to startle Smokin' Joe. He drops the iPod, which falls to the floor pulling his headphones with it. He collapses to the ground beside it, sobbing into a large bunch of weeds.

Fibonacci! My stomach feels hard and uncomfortable as we listen to him wailing.

"It was me ... I did it ... At least I think I did. It was me! ... Or maybe it wasn't? Waaaaaah!"

Is this a clue or is Smokin' Joe Slater yet another person going completely mad?

Porter shifts from foot to foot, opening his mouth to speak but saying nothing. Holly picks up the iPod and leans forward to return it to Smokin' Joe. I grab her arm. The iPod would probably stop him crying, but during the Case of the Exploding Loo we learned that it's usually a good idea to remove people's earphones if they're behaving oddly.

"Maybe it's not him," I say.

Holly pokes Joe with her finger. "Looks like him to me."

"No. I mean maybe Smokin' Joe had nothing to do with the disappearing Space Rock."

"But the girl in the gift shop said—"

"Look at him." I crouch beside the snotty heap of wailing bully. "He hasn't a clue, have you, Joe?"

Smokin' Joe wipes away mucus. "Dunnowhachatalkinbout."

"Someone messed with his brain in the Science Museum," I say. "It was hard to work out what they'd done at first, because he didn't have much of a brain to start with. But seeing the effects up close, I'm sure they zapped him with the negative brain ray, not the positive one. This isn't his—"

WALLOP!

"Owww!" I scream, crashing to the floor beside Smokin' Joe.

I roll on to my back and stare up into the wild eyes of Ma Slater. She's armed with a large iron frying pan and pulls her arm back, ready to strike again.

Raising my hands in surrender, I wiggle backwards, pushing desperately at the weeds with my feet. "Mercy! Mercy!"

"I won't have you bullying my boy, you hear me?" she shrieks, bringing the frying pan down terrifyingly close to my left ear.

"I hear you! I hear you!" If I wasn't in danger of being lobotomised by a frying pan, the idea of *me* bullying Smokin' Joe would be funny. "I'm not bullying him. I'm trying to help him. Please don't frying pan me again, Mrs Slater."

Ma Slater squints at me, then swivels to brandish the frying pan at Holly. "You saying it was this one?" She peers closely at my sister. "Hey, I know you. Yer that Hawkins toe-rag what put my Joe in a wheelie bin a few months back."

Porter takes his life into his own hands by grabbing Ma Slater's pan arm as I try to reason with her.

"Holly only put Joe in the bin to stop him shoving me in there."

"My Joe wouldn't hurt a fly. If you was in that bin, you musta got there by accident."

"Forty-three times?"

"Don't you go confusing me with numbers," Ma Slater screeches, shaking Porter off and raising her arm above her head to give the frying pan greater momentum.

"Afternoon, all," a warm voice greets us. "Making the kids a spot of breakfast, Tracy?"

PC Eric! Perfect timing.

The crazed expression vanishes from Ma Slater's face. She drops her pan arm and smiles like a woman who wasn't about to batter two innocent schoolgirls to mush in her own front yard.

"PC Eric!" she trills. "Fancy a custard cream?"

"Not today thanks, Tracy."

"Not any day." Aggressive Policeman steps out from behind the hedge. "No wonder it takes so long to get anything done out here in the sticks. You're too busy wasting your time munching biscuits with scumbags."

"Who you calling a scumbag?" Ma Slater raises the frying pan, but PC Eric gently takes it from her.

"No need to get excited, Tracy. My colleague doesn't mean to be disrespectful. We just want a quick word with Joe."

"Well you can't have one. Look at the poor beggar. These kids got the lad all upset."

PC Eric pats Joe sympathetically.

Aggressive Policeman prods Joe with his foot and then growls in disgust as he realises his shoe is covered in snot. He looks round for something to wipe it on.

"You!" he says, when he spots me.

"Me," I agree, hoping he's not identifying me as a human handkerchief. "Why so far from London, sir?"

"Not that it's any of your business, but I'm here to talk to this half-wit." He points at Smokin' Joe and snaps his fingers at PC Eric. "Come along, officer. And bring that lump with you."

"Ain't you listening?" Ma Slater blocks the way, large hands on wide hips. "I said he's not going nowhere!"

Aggressive Policeman shoves her towards the house. "No, *you* listen, Mrs Scumbag. I'm talking to that boy whether you like it or not. We can do it here or we can do it down the station."

"Don't upset yourself, Tracy." PC Eric takes Ma Slater's arm. "Let's take this inside. We just want to have a little chat with Joe. Show him a film."

"Film?" Smokin' Joe looks up. His eyes are still glazed, but they seem clearer than they were five minutes ago. "I like films."

Aggressive Policeman yanks him to his feet by his shirt collar. "You'll love this one. It's a hot new release with you in the starring role." He hustles Joe indoors, closely followed by PC Eric and Ma Slater.

Porter glances at the broken front window. "We'll be able to hear everything from here."

"Only if we stay out of sight." Holly presses herself against the wall beneath the window.

Porter and I slither across to join her, hidden from view by tall weeds and piles of rubbish.

10

Up Periscope

It's noon. I don't need a watch to tell me; my stomach likes routine and is now announcing it's time for lunch.

"Shh!" Holly glares at me.

"It's not my fault. We should have bought snacks."

"I'll bring hotdogs to go with the show next time, shall I?" Holly asks.

"That would be nice."

Holly gives me a dead arm. It seems she was being sarcastic.

People aren't getting on much better *inside* the house. Grunts and muttered insults drift through the window until Aggressive Policeman bellows that everyone needs to shut up *now*!

Aggressive Policeman:	**Joe Slater, we are formally charging you with aiding and abetting in the theft of a priceless piece of Moon Rock.**
Ma Slater:	No, you flaming ain't.
Aggressive Policeman:	**We'll be taking your fingerprints and DNA, and we'll need the trainers and the clothes you were wearing at the Science Museum.**
Ma Slater:	Don't give 'em nuffink, Joe.
Smokin' Joe:	I did it.
Ma Slater:	Oh no he didn't.
Aggressive Policeman:	**Oh yes he did.**
PC Eric:	Ahem ... Can you tell us how you did it, Joe?
Smokin' Joe:	Dunno. Just did.
Ma Slater:	Shut up, Joey. My boy ain't done nuffink. You got no proof.
Aggressive Policeman:	**That's where you're wrong. Watch this ...**

I hear the faint whirring of ageing electronic equipment and wish I could see the film footage. But Aggressive Policeman will probably take samples of our DNA too if he sees us peering in through the window. Ooh! I have the solution. I scramble across the Slaters' yard on my hands and knees.

"What are you doing?" Holly hisses. "You'll cut yourself on the broken glass."

"It's the broken glass I need!" I crawl back, waving a juice carton and a few shards of mirror in triumph. I try to fix them in the right position.

"A periscope?" Porter shifts closer, looking impressed. "Cool." He's less impressed by my DIY skills. "Pass it here, sausage fingers, and tell me what to do."

I hand over my wannabe-periscope, not bothering to protest about the 'sausage fingers' comment. I know how to do things in theory but they never work in practice, whereas Porter is Mr Make and Do.

"I need a few more things before we start," I say. "Holly, can you grab those bits of screwed-up newspaper?"

Holly gives me one of her looks, but does as I ask. I pull a stub of pencil out of my pocket and start scribbling a diagram on the old newspaper. It's something I remember seeing on the internet.

JUICE CARTON PERISCOPE

1. Cut the side of a juice carton.

2. Tape two pocket mirrors at a 45 degree angle (A & B).

3. Cut two peek holes (C & D).

4. Tape the flap back.

I have to adapt a bit. The guy who made the diagram clearly wasn't hiding in someone's front yard without scissors or sticky tape.

The bottom of the periscope is easy enough. I get Porter to rest the lower mirror shard on a piece of crumpled newspaper. The top mirror is more complicated. How can I fix it in place?

"We could make homemade glue by mixing a cup of flour, a third of a cup of sugar, a cup and a half of water and a teaspoon of vinegar," I say, uncertainly.

Holly pokes me with a stick. "We're in the Slaters' yard, not a bakery."

"Maybe tree sap would work as a glue substitute." I eye the tree hopefully.

"Enough stupid ideas." Holly snatches the carton from Porter. "Just hold it with your finger."

"Ah. Finger. Yes that'll work."

Porter sniggers. "Remember that story about NASA spending millions to develop a pen that could get ink on to paper without gravity, while the Russians just used pencils?"

"That is a myth," I say with dignity. "And even if it wasn't, I'd be on NASA's side. What if the tip of the pencil broke off and started floating around the space capsule? It could have someone's eye out. Or hit a vital space-button. Give me the million-dollar space pen every time."

"Forget space pens." Holly points our periscope upwards so we can see the TV. "Check out 'Exploring Space'!"

We bunch together so we can see. Porter and Holly bump heads with a thud that echoes through the yard. We press closer to the wall as Ma Slater sticks her large, mullet-haired head out the window.

"Can't see nuffink," she yells. "Must be them big rats again."

Pythagoras! I try not to think about giant rats as I peer into the periscope and watch the Science Museum's security-camera footage.

11

The Hairspray Thief

Building the periscope from scratch takes a few minutes, so we miss the beginning of the footage, but Ma Slater's yawns suggest we haven't missed anything important. As we start watching, the 'Exploring Space' gallery fills with people who've come to find out what's causing the engine noises.

14:59:12   Smokin' Joe clutches his head, and blood trickles from his nose. Remarkable Student Alexander pats his shoulder, subtly pushing him forwards.

15:01:03   Smokin' Joe runs back and forth like a wind-up toy, knocking into exhibits and setting off alarms.

15:03:59 While everyone's distracted by the chaos, Smokin' Joe reaches into his backpack and pulls out a spray can.

Ma Slater smacks her son on the side of the head. "That's my bleedin' hairspray, Joe. I've bin lookin' everywhere fer that."

15:04:42 Smokin' Joe shoots the hairspray high into the air, missing his hair and coating the camera above him in an oily mist. Everything goes blurry as the hairspray settles over the lens.

I peer through the periscope at the screen. My brain is tingling.

CLUE 19
There's something missing
from the screen footage.
Something or someone.

Before I have a chance to work out what, or who, isn't there, Aggressive Policeman clicks the TV off.

There is an uncomfortable silence. I half expect Aggressive Policeman to shout, "Ta-da!"

"That don't prove nuffink," Ma Slater says stubbornly. "What's my boy supposed to have done wrong, other than nick my flamin' hairspray?" Ma Slater wallops Smokin' Joe again.

Aggressive Policeman gets huffy and puffy and big bad wolfy. "Even if we ignore his clear involvement with the theft of the Moon Rock, *madam*, vandalism is a statutory offence that can be prosecuted under criminal law."

"Y'what?"

"Your son has recklessly damaged property belonging to the Science Museum, making him guilty of the offence of vandalism. Not to mention covering the camera lens with hairspray in an obvious attempt to obstruct our investigation."

"I don't see nuffink obvious about it."

Smokin' Joe blinks as if he's coming out of a stupor. "I don't remember what happened," he mumbles, "but I did it. Didn't I?"

"Don't go changing your story now, toe-rag." Aggressive Policeman grabs the front of Smokin' Joe's shirt.

PC Eric puts a restraining arm on Aggressive Policeman's shoulder. "Let the boy speak. There's something not right about all this."

I give a little air-punch. PC Eric never lets me down.

Aggressive Policeman, in contrast, is a permanent disappointment. He's like a human version of the chocolate-grabber machines you get in motorway service stations, which never grab anything except out-of-date Snickers. I hate Snickers.

Aggressive Policeman drags Smokin' Joe towards the front door, declaring, "I'm taking our friend here to the station."

"Not yet," PC Eric protests. "I need another look at that film footage."

"You *are* joking?" Aggressive Policeman stops less than a metre from our periscope (and our heads). "You want to stay *here*?"

Ma Slater takes advantage of their confrontation to snatch back her frying pan and grab a poker from the filthy fireplace. It's a good look. Kind of Medieval Knight during Weapon Shortage.

Using Smokin' Joe as a human shield, Aggressive Policeman edges around her and runs for the police car, dragging Joe with him. He's too busy wrestling with Joe to look back at the Slaters' front yard, so we're safe. For now.

PC Eric moves slower, but thinks faster.

"I had a feeling you'd still be here," he says when he spots us huddled beneath the windowsill. He moves so he's blocking us from view before calling to Aggressive Policeman, "You go on ahead with the patrol car. I've got a few things to sort out here."

Growling in irritation, Aggressive Policeman takes a minute to:

1. Tell PC Eric he's a disgrace to the force
2. Tell Smokin' Joe that annoying a police officer is a crime punishable by death
3. Tell himself he's superior officer material and shouldn't be wasting his time with scumbags

Then he slams the car door and accelerates away.

PC Eric stoops to pick up our juice-carton-periscope. "Ingenious. So you saw the security footage?"

Porter and Holly say nothing.

I nod and wait to be told off.

"Good," PC Eric congratulates me instead. "What did you think?"

"I think I'd like to see it again," I tell him. "Ideally not through a juice carton."

I'd also like to listen to Smokin' Joe's turquoise iPod, which is still in my pocket. (That's not stealing, by the way. It's borrowing. Sort of.)

PC Eric nods. "I'd like to see the footage again too. That shouldn't be a problem. My colleague left in such a hurry he forgot to take it with him."

"Perhaps we could watch it at our house?" I suggest. The crashes we can hear coming from the Slaters' living room suggest Ma Slater is frying-panning everything within reach.

"I'll have to retrieve it from Tracy Slater." PC Eric doesn't look keen. "You three might want to wait out here. I'm going inside and may be some time."

12

Caught On Camera

PC Eric emerges from the Slaters' house waving the USB drive like a knight flourishing the (very small) head of a conquered dragon.

Holly and I cheer, but not too loudly. We haven't forgotten the Frying Pan of Pain.

As we cross the road, I notice Porter lagging behind. "You coming to watch?"

"Nah." He takes another step backwards. "Stuff to do. Catch you later."

"Stuff to do?" Holly folds her arms. "Since when do you have stuff to do?"

"Since now," Porter says, shuffling off into the distance.

"That's the third time he's vanished in as many days," Holly says. "I'm starting to think Porter

Grimm is his mild-mannered alter-ego and he's leading a secret double life."

I rub my arms, which have suddenly gone cold. "Both his identities could be good though, right?"

Holly clears her throat but says nothing. She's been weird with Porter ever since Gift Shop Girl.

I decide to pretend she's joking, because I don't like the alternative. "What's Porter's secret identity then? News Re-Porter? Space Porter-l?"

"Arsenal Su-Porter?" Holly adds with a reluctant grin.

"Isn't he a portaloo spotter?" PC Eric asks, and it takes me a minute to realise he's not playing the secret identity game. "Maybe that's what he's doing when he disappears."

I shake my head as I push open our front door. "Porter always comes back from portaloo spotting trips with a load of film for us to watch. He hasn't made us look at anything recently. Thank *Fermat*."

Mum looks up as we enter the living room and blinks in confusion when she spots PC Eric.

"Hello, Mrs Hawkins," he says softly, holding out his hand.

She uses it to lever herself off the sofa. "Cup of tea?"

Holly and I stop mid-stride. I try to remember the last time Mum got up to greet a visitor. It was months ago – before Ms Grimm zapped her with the negative brain ray and transformed her into a sofa-sloth. The doctors say the stupidifying effects should have worn off by now, but Mum still prefers to view life from the couch. She doesn't even get up for her old friend the milkman any more, because 'Dad wouldn't like it'. Although she's happy enough for us to let the milkman in when a light bulb needs changing or something needs fixing.

But Mum is on her feet now, trudging through to the kitchen. She returns with a chipped mug, which she hands to PC Eric before sinking back on to the sofa with a sigh.

I set up the security footage while PC Eric sips at

his tea unenthusiastically. After a minute, he reaches into his cup and pulls out two teabags, a pencil sharpener and a cocktail umbrella.

"Sorry," Holly mutters, "Mum's not fully recovered from the negative brain ray."

"No problem." PC Eric twiddles his cocktail umbrella. "The tea was a nice thought and the pencil sharpenings added an interesting texture. It's good to see your mum again. She was on my mind while I was listening to Joe Slater earlier. What do you think of his behaviour recently?"

This is why I love PC Eric. He makes connections.

"You think Joe's being brainwashed like Mum was?" I'm tempted to tell him I might have the proof in my pocket, but I want to hear whose voice is on the iPod before I share it. "Let's watch the film footage again. It might give us a clue."

PC Eric puts the film on. I lean closer to the TV at the part where Smokin' Joe pulls the hairspray out of his backpack. I have that same feeling there's something's missing from the shot, but I still can't figure out what it is. It's like a grey blanket has been thrown over my memory.

I ask PC Eric to run the footage in slow motion. I can't suppress a smug smile when it reveals I was right when I said Joe couldn't have taken the Space Rock.

"See?" I challenge Holly.

"Didn't doubt you for a minute," she replies. "But look at Smokin' Joe! What's wrong with him?"

On-Screen Joe is acting weirdly, even by his own standards. Something is bothering him and he keeps lifting his hand to his earphones.

I need to listen to that iPod.

I pat my pocket to make sure the iPod is still inside and announce, "I'm just nipping to the loo."

I perch on the toilet seat and press 'play'.

"You will tell everyone you are responsible for the theft."

I know that voice.

The rush of relief is stronger than I expected. It's not Dad! I can give the iPod to PC Eric now. Well, maybe not *right now*. Maybe I could listen to the rest of it first? The brain ray can't be on 'zap' mode because my head feels fine. I turn Remarkable Student Alexander back on:

"'I did it'. That's all you have to say. 'I did it! I can't remember what happened, but I know I did it.' Say it after me: 'I did it! I did it!' That's all you have to do to receive fifty pounds and a date with Holly Hawkins ..."

I splutter. Smokin' Joe's prize is a date with my sister? "Holly! Come here! You have to hear this."

"I don't want to hear anything you're doing in the toilet, thank you very much."

"Urgh. No. I meant you should hear this iPod." I race back to the living room. "You too, PC Eric."

PC Eric looks up. "First I have a couple of questions about one of the young men in your group – Alexander West."

I hold out the iPod. "Then you definitely want to listen to this."

"That's Smokin' Joe's iPod!" Holly hisses. She subtly waggles her head towards PC Eric before adding, "I'm sure you haven't been listening to it, because that would be illegal or something."

PC Eric puts up a hand to stop me replying. "Perhaps you found it on the ground and, not being sure who it belonged to, you listened to it briefly before handing it to a passing policeman?"

I nod, embracing my inner big fat liar, and hand the machine to PC Eric. "Remarkable Student Alexander is responsible for the Space Rock's disappearance. This proves it."

PC Eric strokes his chin. "I had my suspicions after reading your witness statement, but the CCTV footage, fuzzy as it is, suggests he's innocent."

"Put the film footage on again," I say. "Maybe I'll spot something."

But PC Eric's right. Even though the images are blurred after Smokin' Joe's hairspray attack, it's clear Remarkable Student Alexander is too far away to have taken the Space Rock. However, when we freeze the frame, he seems to be deliberately blocking the camera. When he moves, the Rock is gone.

"He's involved," I insist. "I know he is."

PC Eric shrugs. "Perhaps. But we have no real evidence to prove it."

"Yes we do." I plug Smokin' Joe's iPod into the speaker. Holly and PC Eric listen quietly until we get to the bit about Smokin' Joe's reward.

"A date with me?" Holly retches. "Over my dead body!"

PC Eric keeps replaying the iPod message. Holly

gags each time it reaches the end, which gets annoying pretty quickly.

After the fifth re-play, PC Eric says, "Notice anything about the boy's voice?"

I ignore Holly's fake-puking and focus on Alexander's words. "He's reading!" I realise. "Is that what you mean?"

CLUE 22
Remarkable Student Alexander
is reading from a script.

PC Eric beams. "Clever girl!"

"And you think he wasn't the one who wrote the words?"

PC Eric gives me a proud nod. "Even cleverer girl!"

So who did write them?

"Are there lots of people who might want to steal a Space Rock?" I ask, keen to clear Dad's name for this crime – in my own head at least.

"I suppose so. Moon Rocks are worth a lot of money. But they're hard to sell. And now we know the dangers I don't understand why anyone would still want to keep this one." PC Eric gives me a policeman look – jaw set, chin high, no blinking. "Do you have a reason for asking?"

"No. Just curious."

I love PC Eric but there are some suspicions I want to keep to myself for now.

13

Schnookums

"What about the dodgy camera?" Holly asks PC Eric. "We heard a security camera blacked out in 'Investigating Alien Worlds'. Do you have any footage of what was happening before it went blank?"

"Only on the computer we set up back at the station for the officer from the London Metropolitan Police. I can't get you access to that."

"Don't worry, PC Eric." Holly jumps to her feet. "I have a plan."

PC Eric didn't look worried before. But he does now. Especially when Holly grabs him and bundles him into a taxi, ordering the cabbie to take us to "Butt's Hill Police Station, please."

"Are you expecting me to give you a guided

tour?" he asks as we clamber out of the taxi and enter the police station

"Won't be necessary." Holly pushes past PC Eric and launches herself at the desk sergeant. "I need to see my darling boyfriend," she announces. "And I need to see him *now*!"

My mouth drops open. What *darling boyfriend*?

"My little Joey was dragged to this police station against his wishes," Holly stamps her foot. "That's kidnapping. I want to make a complaint against that nasty police officer from London."

The desk sergeant gives an involuntary nod at 'nasty police officer', leading me to conclude Aggressive Policeman is not popular here either. No wonder, if he treats everyone the way he treats PC Eric.

A plan begins to form.

"Shh, Holly," I stage-whisper, loud enough for the desk sergeant to hear. "We annoyed the London policeman so much we'll never be allowed near him again. They won't want us to upset him."

The desk sergeant strokes his chin.

PC Eric's lips twitch. "You have a point there, NOELLE HAWKINS." He booms my name in what I assume is an unflattering attempt to remind the desk sergeant of my reputation as annoyer-of-policemen. "I don't suppose I'll be able to give you that station tour after all."

The desk sergeant bites his lip. "Well, Eric, if you promised the girls—"

We charge into the main police station before he has a chance to finish his sentence.

"Oi! Police people! Where's my boyfriend?" Holly tosses her hair like the girl in the museum gift shop and skips through the cubicles calling, "Joey? Schnookums? Where are you?"

PC Eric subtly nudges us forward and to the right, until we reach the desk where Aggressive Policeman and Smokin' Joe are sitting, scowling at each other. Behind them is a computer screen showing footage of the Science Museum.

Holly launches herself at Smokin' Joe and wraps her arms around his neck.

"Ooof," Smokin' Joe splutters and then breaks into a grin that makes his head look like an over-carved Halloween pumpkin.

Holly narrows her eyes at me over Smokin' Joe's shoulder.

"What?" Oh, yes, I'm supposed to be finding the security footage from before the camera cut out. But how? Aggressive Policeman is right next to the computer. I may be good with technology, but I'm not invisible. I try to signal to Holly, but she's too busy smacking Smokin' Joe's hands to notice.

"Ahem!" I cough. "Maybe you want to take all the love stuff *outside*!"

Holly gets the message and rises to her feet, pulling Smokin' Joe by the hand. He follows willingly.

"Hey!" Aggressive Policeman strides after them. "No one said you could leave."

"You can't keep my little Joey here without his mummy." Holly snuggles up to all ten tonnes of 'little Joey' with only a tiny shudder. "I think I saw Ma Slater outside, with her frying pan. We should send someone to fetch her for you."

Aggressive Policeman makes a choking noise in his throat. "Do not let that woman in," he orders the local police. "Block the entrance. And someone sit that boy back down."

No one moves to help. Aggressive Policeman lunges for Smokin' Joe, grabbing him by the waist. Joe, in turn, clutches at Holly, creating a weird sort of Holly/Joe/Aggressive Policeman conga.

Perfect. The computer is now Aggressive Policeman free. Even better, everyone is watching the strange little dance snaking through the station. Best of all, the computer's still logged on. It doesn't take long to locate the footage and load it on to my USB drive.

Pocketing the drive, I wave across at Holly, who

looks ready to throw up. I'm not surprised, with Smokin' Joe kissing her ear. Urgh. Unpeeling him, she wriggles free and we race towards reception.

"Wait," Smokin' Joe calls after Holly. "Where you going?"

"Sorry, Schnookums," Holly calls back. "It's been fabulous, but I think we should take a break."

"Take a break?" Smokin' Joe lumbers after her. "You have to start something before you can take a break from it! Come back 'ere."

"Over my dead body," Holly mutters and we sprint for the door.

I look at Joe and feel a twinge of sympathy. Everyone's been using him recently and it doesn't seem fair. I shrug apologetically. He makes kissy faces in response. My sympathetic feelings wear off pretty quickly.

"Enjoying your tour so far?" PC Eric appears behind us, blocking Smokin' Joe's approach and giving Aggressive Policeman a chance to catch him.

"Great," I stop to tell him. "I managed to . . ."

PC Eric covers his ears. "I don't think I want to hear what you managed to do. Just keep moving. Your sister seems keen to leave and I can't say I blame her."

Smokin' Joe waggles his tongue at Holly. Ugh.

Double Ugh. He only stops when Aggressive Policeman slaps a hand on his collar.

"Gotcha, scumbag."

"Come on, girls," PC Eric says. "I'll take you home."

14

No Nee Nah

"Can we put the siren on?"

"No."

"Oh go on, PC Eric. Just for a minute? Pleeeeease?"

"Can I save time by explaining that 'no' means 'no'. 'No' does not mean 'if you beg and whine and whinge and wail I'll make it a yes'."

"But—"

"But nothing." PC Eric checks his mirror and indicates left. "One more word about sirens and you can get out and walk – making all the siren noises you like."

"No siren," Holly murmurs sorrowfully.

"No siren," PC Eric agrees. His words are hard but his eyes are smiling, so I risk another question.

"What will happen to Smokin' Joe now?"

"I've entered his iPod into evidence," PC Eric replies, changing gear to turn the corner. "So, I imagine they'll speak to Alexander West and decide how to proceed after that."

"Remarkable Student Alexander is a snake," I say. "You should have seen what he was like in the museum. The police believed everything he said."

"We need to get to him first," Holly says.

"I didn't hear that." PC Eric puts his foot on the brake as we reach our road.

"We need to scare him into telling us the truth."

"Definitely didn't hear that."

"Dad's chainsaw's still in the garage," Holly adds.

"I've suddenly gone completely deaf." PC Eric pulls into the kerb. "Just don't do anything stupid. You won't be able to solve anything if you're hauled down to the station."

"We need a way to intimidate Alexander without getting ourselves into trouble," Holly tells me as we clamber out of the patrol car.

"We need Porter." I miss our third head.

"No we don't." Holly almost sounds like she means it. "You're the one with the Sherlock brain. Use it."

I try to think, but a loud, rhythmic smashing sound on the other side of the street keeps breaking my concentration. *"Tim Berners Lee!* What is that noise?"

"It's Ma Slater." Holly giggles. "She's frying-panning the big tree in her yard."

"If the tree falls, it'll crush her house. That woman's as mad as an armadillo," I say. "She scares me."

"She scares everyone." Holly says. "Oooh ..."

A metaphorical light bulb appears in the air between us. As one, we march across the road. PC Eric rolls down the car window and calls after us. "Remember. Nothing stupid?"

Okay, this plan definitely comes under 'stupid', but it has to be worth a try. We reach the Slaters' front yard and I look across at Holly. She looks back at me. Ma Slater spots us while we're trying to glare each other into speaking first.

"Want some of this?" She waves the frying pan at us.

"Er, no thank you. We just wanted to let you know how Joe's doing."

"You seen my boy?" She rests the frying pan against the tree.

I nod, keeping my eyes on the pan. "We know who's been making him do all these crazy things – a boy called Alexander West."

"West?" she screeches. "I know his mother –

stuck-up old bat. Thinks her toilets smell of roses. Wait till I tell her what I think of that son of hers." She seizes the pan and storms down the road, taking a few practice swings at lampposts.

Holly and I jog along behind her.

"We've created a monster," I murmur.

"Nah. She was already a monster," Holly says. "We've just given the monster a mission!"

Ma Slater stops abruptly outside a smart semi-detached house with perfectly pruned trees and a pathway lined with potted plants. Or, at least, it *was* lined with potted plants. Now Mad Ma Slater is taking her frying pan to them. After annihilating the pot plants, she starts smashing through the white PVC front door.

15

Ma Slater Smash

The door is dead. I look at Holly in alarm, but she just shrugs and follows Ma Slater into the house. A woman in a checked apron steps out of the kitchen to protest. I stare at her in astonishment; she looks like an illustration of a mother in an old fairy tale with her rosy cheeks and perfectly groomed hair.

"Hello," I mumble, rooted to the spot. "We've just popped round to see Alexander."

Holly is already halfway up the stairs and reaches through the bannisters to give me a shake. "Being polite is a good thing, Know-All, but Ma Slater has already smashed their pot plants to smithereens, battered down their front door and knocked chunks out of their staircase. The politest thing we can do at this point is make sure she doesn't kill anybody. So GET UP HERE, NOW!"

I rub my eyes and follow orders. Nothing seems real. It's the combination of the Wests' perfectly ordered house and the insane hurricane of Ma Slater's fury. She's found a set of china figurines on the landing and is leaning over the top bannister, crushing them, one by one, in her giant fists. She's too deep in the crazy zone to hear the voices at the other end of the landing but Holly and I creep closer to the conversation.

"No one told us the Space Rock could hurt people." Remarkable Student Shazia's voice wavers. "I read in the paper that the NASA scientists who were exposed to the American rock tried to eat each other before their brains exploded."

Holly shoots me a questioning look. We've been competing to find the craziest newspaper story about the effects of the Space Rock. Sounds like we've found a winner. I'm pretty sure most of the stories are made up, but they say there's no smoke without fire. And if exploding brains are the smoke then I'm not keen to feel the fire.

We have to solve this case quickly and get the Space Rock back where it belongs.

Remarkable Student Shazia is still talking. "We should tell the police what we know."

"That would be like admitting we're responsible."
That's Remarkable Student Omar. "We can't be held
responsible for this."

"We are not responsible." Remarkable Student
Alexander's voice contains none of his friends'
panic or uncertainty. "We were just following
orders."

His words freeze me to the spot.

They have the opposite effect on Holly. She blazes
into the room. "That's what the Nazis said!" She
pokes Alexander in the chest. "You big, posh Nazi."

"Holly Hawkins!" He sounds amused. "Here in
my home and as charming as ever. I wondered who
was causing all the noise. Where are Tweedledum
and Tweedledumber? He pokes his head through
the door and grabs me by the hood. "Ha. Here's one
of them. So, where's the other idiot?"

I wish I knew. Porter should be here. We're a
team. Ma Slater's a bad substitute – too dangerous
and smashy. I stare into Remarkable Student
Alexander's smug face and an evil idea floats into
my head.

"Why don't you call for him?" I suggest. "You
could try yelling, 'We're in here, idiot!' That should
do it."

"It's not often I follow your advice, Hawkins,"
Alexander says, "but this time I just might. Idi-o-t,"

he calls as if coaxing a cat. "Where are you? Here, thicky thicky. Here, thicky thicky."

He sticks his head round the door.

Big mistake. Seconds later it bounces back into the room with a resounding 'Thwack!'

"Who you calling 'thick', you snotty-nosed brat?" Ma Slater throws her frying pan at him, and I half expect it to fly back to her hand like Thor's hammer. "What did you do to my boy?"

Remarkable Student Alexander doesn't answer. He just bends over and clutches his head.

With a roar of rage, Ma Slater grabs the pan and wallops him from behind, sending him sprawling headfirst on to his bed. Shazia reaches out to pat him sympathetically, but doesn't get too close. I guess she's worried he might mess up her white jeans.

Ma Slater spots her and Omar for the first time. "More snooty kids." She glowers at them and lifts the frying pan. "Are you part of this?"

"No!" Shazia quickly withdraws her hand from Alexander's shoulder.

Omar raises his arms in surrender, angling his fingers so they're pointing at Alexander. "Nothing to do with us. Just him."

"I've done nothing wrong. Owwwww!" Alexander rolls around on the bed, clutching his

head, then his leg, then his head. "I was just following orders from our old headmistress."

Wait! What?

Holly and I look at each other. He can't mean ...

"Ms Grimm."

16

Grimm Reality

"Goodbye Remarkable Students Alexander, Shazia and Omar," I say as Holly grabs my hand and drags me out of Alexander's room.

We bump into Mr and Mrs West on the stairs. Fortunately for us (less so for their son) Remarkable Student Alexander gives another howl of frying-pan-induced pain and they push past us to get to him, leaving our exit free.

Holly races from the house as if Smokin' Joe was hot on her heels. "Come on!" she calls. "We need to watch that security footage."

I follow at more of an asthmatic trot, taking in the aftermath of Ma Slater's destruction – massacred pot plants, brutalised traffic cones and slightly wonky lampposts. When we reach home, I head straight for my room and make my way through my to-scale Meccano solar system to insert the USB drive in my computer. Wheezing like a maltreated donkey, I collapse on to my bed.

Less than thirty seconds later, I leap up again.

"*Archimedes!*" I stroke Saturn's rings and stare at the image frozen on screen. "The Remarkable Students were telling the truth. It's Ms Grimm! The hair's different and she's wearing glasses, but it's definitely her."

Ms Grimm. The Grimm Reaper. The Brains behind LOSERS. The monster that stupidified Mum. The criminal who disappeared before the police could question her about child kidnapping and brainwashing. And now, apparently, Dad's mysterious museum volunteer.

CLUE 23
Ms Grimm has been caught on camera
at the Science Museum.

So she's no longer 'missing, whereabouts unknown'. Shame the same can't be said for Porter. Does he know his mother's back on the scene? Is she the reason for his disappearance?

I try his mobile. No answer.

"Trying to call Porter?" Holly fiddles with my Meccano model of Mercury, knowing it annoys me. "He's probably sitting with the Grimm Reaper, staring at the caller ID, wondering what we know."

"I'm wondering the same thing." I try not to think about Holly's dirty fingerprints on Mercury. "What *do* we know?"

"We know Porter's keeping secrets," Holly says. "We know Ms Grimm's involved in the Science Museum heist. We know we only have eleven days to find the Moon Rock before brains start exploding. And we know we should stop calling it the 'Moon' Rock because it could come from anywhere ... Maybe from here." She touches my Meccano Mars. "Or here." She pokes Venus. "Or he—"

"Stop it!" I yell, grabbing her hands.

To be fair, she might be right. Meteorites from Mars were found in the Antarctic, so it's possible they also hit the moon. And meteorites from Venus might affect the human brain. Being closer to the sun, Venus lacks Earth's geomagnetic protection field and its rocks are constantly blasted by high-energy radiation. But that doesn't mean it's okay for Holly to fiddle with my Meccano.

"Touch one more planet and I'll start poking and prodding *you*. See how you like it."

"Touchy." Holly pulls her hands free, restarts the CCTV footage and pretends to reach for Neptune.

"NO touchy!" I smack her hand. "That's my point!"

But my concern for my Meccano planets is forgotten moments later. *"Fibonacci!"*

Holly reaches out to touch the screen. "How did we miss that?"

Good question.

CLUE 24

Wrapped in tin foil, in plain view,
on the top of the Mars lander
is something that looks very much
like the missing brain ray.

17

Foiled

"Another lift to the Science Museum?" Uncle Max grumbles as Holly forces her way into his car. "What do you think I am? Your personal taxi service? And where's the lodger?"

"Missing in action. You're going to London anyway," Holly says. "I heard you say so on the phone. Surely you can give your two favourite nieces a lift?"

"You're my *only* nieces."

"Which means you have plenty of free time to chauffeur us around."

When Uncle Max looks ready to refuse, Holly smiles with all her teeth. "I've been wondering what you *do* on these trips to London, Uncle Max? Perhaps I should ask Aunty Vera?"

I look up in surprise. Vigil-Aunty doesn't know

about his visits to London? How is that possible? She has eyes everywhere. Although, now I think about it, she hasn't been her usual scary self lately. She'll be fifty at the end of the month and it's obviously bothering her because she won't let anyone use the 'f-word' (fifty) and insists she's turning forty-nine B.

She has become obsessed with watching old *Star Wars* movies. Apparently, she was always a fan of the actor who plays Han Solo and, on her wedding day, Uncle Max gave her special permission to kiss the Han Solo man if she met him in real life. Aunty Vera is worried she's becoming too old to take advantage of that deal.

In an attempt to cheer Aunty Vera up, I pointed

Hans Solo

Princess Leia

gold bikini

out that she has *more* chance of getting her kiss now, because Han Solo Man must be at least seventy so he probably can't run as fast.

Vigil-Aunty hit me with her handbag.

"Should I ask her, Uncle Max?" Holly is saying. "Should I ask Aunty Vera what you're up to?"

"Just get in," he growls. "But next time you pay petrol money."

"Love you too, Uncle Max."

Despite Holly badgering him all the way to London ('badgering' as in 'asking something repeatedly' not 'digging tunnels and eating earthworms'), Uncle Max refuses to reveal where he's going. I tell myself not to care. I have enough mysteries to solve without worrying about what Uncle Max is up to.

Holly and I know the layout of the Science Museum now, so we march straight to the spot in the 'Exploring Space' gallery where the security footage showed the brain ray. How could I have missed it? It's like they say, 'the best hiding place is in full view' (although they should have added 'wrapped in tin foil'). My hands shake as we approach the Mars lander. To discover ... nothing.

CLUE 25
The brain ray has vanished.

"*Hypatia!* What now?" I ask Holly.

Holly kicks the barrier.

"What now, other than kicking things?" I ask. "We've got two hours to find the Space Rock, the brain ray *and* the Grimm Reaper. Suggestions?"

"We need to figure this out," Holly says. "Let's take it in turns to act out stealing the Space Rock and brain ray to work out how it was done."

In the end, all we manage to figure out is that the thefts should have been impossible.

CLUE 26
To leave the gallery carrying the Space Rock, brain ray or both, you would have to walk past at least one functioning security camera.

"'*Francis Crick!* This makes no sense," I say. "We've watched the security footage. We would have seen them. There is only one way the Space Rock could have left this place."

Holly looks at me expectantly.

"It was stolen by the Invisible Man."

Holly kicks me.

"Oww! Is that your way of telling me the Space Rock would still be visible even if the Invisible Man wasn't? Do you think it would become invisible if the Invisible Man ate it? Or stuffed it up his—"

I'm interrupted by a crash on the other side of 'Exploring Space'. The distraction is probably a good thing as Holly's kicking leg is still swinging.

Across by the Apollo lander, the tall security guard I spoke to on my last visit whips back his arm to punch his fellow guard in the face. His aim is good but his colleague has incredible reflexes and steps back a split second before the fist makes contact, so it just skims his jaw. Stumbling slightly, the second guard lifts his left hand to his face and hits out at Tall Guard with the right. Tall blocks the move effortlessly as if he knew it was coming.

Grunting in frustration, Other Guard hooks his leg around Tall's knees in an attempt to bring him to the ground, but he's not fast enough and Tall steps out of harm's way. The two men dart back and forth, aiming and dodging kicks and punches as if the moves have been choreographed beforehand. But they both look too angry to be doing this for show.

Tall jabs at Other, who shifts out of the way milli-seconds before Tall's fist reaches him. They stare at each other intently, circling and matching moves. Tall cracks his knuckles and Other wipes sweat from his face.

"I'm not saying I want them to beat each other up or anything," Holly says. "Okay, maybe I do a little bit," she admits. "But isn't this the weirdest fight you've ever seen? Where's the trash talk? And why can't either of them land a punch?"

"Definitely the weirdest fight," I agree. "This place gets freakier each time we visit."

It's a relief when Holly's phone buzzes and Uncle Max announces our two hours are up.

18

Lost And Found And Insulted

Halfway home, Holly realises she's left her sunglasses behind. Nice ones too: an old designer pair Mum gave away when she stopped leaving the house.

"Come on, Uncle Max," Holly pleads. "We're only forty minutes away. I love those sunglasses."

"No way. Look at this traffic. And LET GO OF MY ARM! Do you want us to crash?"

"But—"

"But nothing." Uncle Max returns his hands to the ten-to-two position on the steering wheel and stares straight ahead.

"You should call the museum," I tell her. "They must have a Lost Property department."

Holly beams. "You *are* a genius, Know-All! Uncle Max, I need your phone because mine's out of credit."

Uncle Max grumbles about blackmailers, phone thieves and road accidents waiting to happen, but he hands his mobile over.

"Sorry to bother you," Holly says to whoever picks up at the other end. "I don't suppose anyone's handed in a pair of aviator sunglasses? I think I left them in the girls' toilets and— They *have*?" she claps, nearly dropping the phone. "Someone handed them in? Wow! Science Museum people rule! No, I'm in the car on my way home, so I don't know when I'll be able to pick them up, but— You will?" She covers the mouthpiece and hisses, "They'll post them to me. How cool is that?"

I spread my hands to show a large amount of coolness.

"How much will that cost?" Holly asks. "You're joking! It's free? Okay, wait a minute. I'll give you my address ..."

While Holly tries to remember where we live, it occurs to me that this might be a clue:

CLUE 27
Science Museum Lost Property are
prepared to send a lost item, free of charge,
to the address of anyone who claims it.

I grab the phone.

Me:	**"Is it official Lost Property policy to send items to people who lose them?"**
Lost Property Man:	"Yeah."
Me:	**"Even now, with the police checking everything that goes out of the building?"**
Lost Property Man:	"Huh?"
Me:	**"Aren't the police checking your post?"**
Lost Property Man:	"Nah. Not really."
Me:	**"Has anyone asked you to send them a lost rock?"**
Lost Property Man:	" . . . "
Me:	**"Would that be an offended silence?"**

Lost Property Man:	"Yeah. I'm not stupid. I'm hardly gonna go posting stolen Moon Rocks to people, am I? Put the nice girl back on. I need her address."
Me:	**"I can give you that. We live at—"**
Lost Property Man:	"Nah. Don't wanna talk to you. Gimme the nice girl."

Humph. I hand the phone back to Holly, who rattles off our address and giggles at something the Lost Property Muppet says.

I grab the phone back.

Me:	**"Has anyone asked you to send them a brain ray?"**
Lost Property Man:	"If you wanna make prank calls, call someone else."
Me:	**"It's hardly a prank call when she's just told you where I live, is it? Be sensible. Now, has anyone asked you to—?"**

Lost Property Man:	(*Cough*.) "Have you lost any property in the Science Museum?"
Me:	**"No, but—"**
Lost Property Man:	"Then I don't gotta talk to you."

... Dial tone ...

Fine. I don't want to talk to him either. I have a lot to think about.

19

Mum Moves

Holly kicks Uncle Max's car door shut, boots our garden gate open, and karate kicks the front door. And Lost Property Man thinks she's a 'nice girl'? Pah!

"I don't understand why you're kicking things," I say. "I thought you were happy they found your sunglasses."

"I'm multi-emoting. It's a skill. I can be both happy about the sunglasses *and* mad about the brain ray at the same time. Look!" Holly sticks her thumbs in the air with a big grin and then lowers her right hand to punch the living-room door. "*And* I can be deeply suspicious about the timing of Porter's disappearance. What does he know about the brain ray? It was on the Mars lander. We saw it."

"Brain ray?" Mum says from the sofa.

Holly and I jump. Mum spends all day watching TV and not saying a word, so it's easy to forget she's there. That sounds bad, but I think Mum forgets she's there herself sometimes. Maybe it's a brain-ray thing. After having your mind emptied it must be hard to fill it up again. Occasionally, though, something grabs her attention. Today, that thing is the brain ray.

"Are you saying someone stole the brain ray from the Science Museum?" she asks.

"We never mentioned the Science Museum." I take a step back from the sofa. "How do you know it was there?"

Mum speaks slowly as if I'm a bit simple. "I put it there, didn't I?"

Holly and I gawp at her. Synchronised staring. "*You* put it there?"

"Yes. Your dad asked me to."

"Dad asked you to?" I echo.

Mum nods. "When he called me after his arrest, I told him I didn't want that thing sitting in the attic."

"In the attic?"

"Are you going to repeat everything I say?" Mum asks. "I'm sure I remember conversations being slightly more interesting."

"But ... ?" I say.

"But ... ?" Holly continues.

"Ah, yes, much better." Mum's laugh sounds out of practice, reminding me that my conversation skills are being mocked by someone who's barely spoken since Christmas.

"But ... I don't understand." Holly manages to get a full sentence out. "You're saying *you* took the brain ray?"

"I borrowed it and no one asked for it back," Mum replies as if that explains everything.

"You didn't consider handing it in?"

"I didn't know who to trust. I did consider giving it to the milkman, but he didn't seem to want it."

"So you decided to trust Dad?" Holly asks. "The least trustworthy of the lot."

"Don't talk about your father like that," Mum says. "He's not a bad man. Well, not a *really* bad man. He hasn't killed anyone yet."

Holly snorts. "Oh, well, that's all right then."

"He was very helpful about the brain ray. He said it would be safe at the Science Museum if I wrapped it in silver foil and made it part of the space display."

"Seriously?"

"It worked, didn't it?" Mum says. "It's been there for over a month."

"How did you put it there without setting off the sensor?"

Mum pushes herself up from the sofa, pretends to trip, giggles foolishly and talks to an imaginary museum guard. "Ooops. Clumsy old me. I must have leaned too far over the barrier. So sorry, I didn't mean to set off that noisy sensor."

I can see how the security guards would believe she'd made a harmless mistake.

"You went to all that trouble for Dad?"

"No. For all of us. I couldn't bring myself to destroy your father's invention but I didn't want it in the house. The museum seemed the safest place."

"Except it wasn't."

Mum crashes back down on to the sofa. "Yes, there is that."

"So, what do we do now?" I ask.

"Find it," Mum says simply, returning her attention to daytime TV.

20

Lost Toys

Days Left to Save the Earth: 9

'Find it'? Easy to say, but where to start? It feels odd to be investigating without our third head. Porter's been missing for two whole days. If it was term time we'd at least see him at school, but the holidays have started so he could be anywhere. It's yet another thing to worry about and we're in danger of losing focus. The brain ray can't be our main concern; neither can Porter. Not when we only have nine days left to find the missing Moon(ish) Rock and save the Earth from lunar loonies and exploding brains.

Speaking of loonies, Holly is prancing around the living room in her designer sunglasses, which arrived this morning, less than forty-eight hours after she called the Lost Property Muppet to say they were missing.

"I should ring and thank him."

"Wouldn't bother," I grunt. "He was rude."

"Not to me." Holly skips to the telephone.

I have no interest in what the Lost Property Muppet has to say, but I tune in when Holly asks, "Why? What's wrong with them?"

I move closer. "What's wrong with who?"

"Security guys from 'Exploring Space'," Holly mouths.

"What *is* wrong with them?"

Holly covers the bottom of her phone. "They're in intensive care. It may be Space Rock related. One guard was so sick in front of a school tour group yesterday that the kids fled the building, terrified by all those news reports into thinking that his head was about to blow up. My Lost Property friend is complaining they left their toys behind."

I nod. Then I stop nodding. What kind of kid takes a toy on a school trip? And if they're that crazy about their toy, they're not going to leave it behind just because of a bit of projectile vomiting, are they?

I grab the phone. "Did any of these toys look like a space gun? Kind of plastic and turquoise-coloured?"

"Oh. It's you," Lost Property Muppet says without enthusiasm.

"Can you just answer the question?"

Holly snatches the phone back. "Sorry about my sister ..."

"Oi! Don't apologise for me." I'm getting fed up with 'nice' Holly.

" ... But we *are* interested in turquoise space gun toys." Holly flutters her eyelashes. At the phone! I mean, seriously? "I know it's a silly question, but did anyone hand in something like that?" She raises her eyebrows. "They did?"

"*Fibonacci!* Is this guy completely stupid? I asked him about brain rays the other day. Why didn't he call us?"

Holly covers the phone speaker and glares at me. "You. Are. Not. Helping." She removes her hand and continues all nicey nicey. "I don't suppose we could pop in and see it? What ... ? You've already sent it to someone?" She kicks the wall.

That's more like it. Bye bye Mrs Nice Holly.

"Address," I hiss. "We need the address he sent it to."

Holly grabs a pen and my *New Scientist* magazine. "He's not just going to give me someone's address for no reason," she hisses back.

"Then come up with a reason. Fast. And don't even think of writing on my magazine."

Holly scowls, but starts talking. "You've already

sent it? Well, that's a relief. My aunt must have called you after our cousin lost his toy space gun. Can I check the address you've sent it to, just to make sure? Ah. You want me to give you *her* address so you can see if it's the same?" Holly gives a high-pitched laugh and then grabs my arm and mouths, "Help!"

I start thinking. If we believe the brain ray was posted to Ms Grimm and we think Porter's with her, then she can't be far away.

"Ask if it's in Lindon," I whisper.

"Lindon?" Holly says to Lost Property Muppet. "Did my aunt ask you to send it to her Lindon address? ... She did? *Brilliant!*"

I cough.

Holly gives me an apologetic grimace. "I mean, yes, of course, that makes sense. You want the road name? Um, did she give you her Castle Road address? She didn't. Then it must have been the other house. The one on ... um ... Bla– ... no, Dar– ... no, Arl– ... Albion Road? Yes, that's what I was saying. Because that's where she lives. At number ... t – f – s – seven you say? Yes. 7 Albion Road. That'll be it. Thank you very much."

If my suspicions are right, Ms Grimm bought this new place after her rooms at LOSERS were damaged in the fire. She'd have needed somewhere to hide from the police while they investigated the kid-napping and brainwashing accusations against her.

"Right. Let's call PC Eric," Holly says.

"Porter will hate us for doing it," I point out. "We should try and get more proof first."

Holly nods "Yes, you're right. Time to check out 7 Albion Road."

"What?" I stare at her in alarm. "That's not what I meant!"

"Well it should have been. It's a great idea. Come on."

Uh-oh.

21

7 Albion Road

Days Left to Save the Earth: 8

It's just after midnight and the moon is huge. Wispy clouds form freaky moon-fingers that point down at 7 Albion Road. The scene looks like a spooky screenshot from a horror movie. The shot they play the dur-duh-dur-duh-dur-duh music over, warning you to flee while you still can. The shot they show just before all the bad stuff happens.

And in the corner of this shot, Holly and I lurk behind a large skip, planning our break-in.

My heart slams against my ribs as something leaps from among the rubbish in the skip. "Cat," I tell myself, "It's just a cat." But that doesn't stop my heart beating out, "Monster! Axe murderer! Zombie!"

Zombie Cat

Cat

Axe-Murdering Cat

I glare at Holly, who looks barely human in the darkness. "Remind me why I let you talk me into this."

"Because you know we have to find the brain ray." Holly strokes the zombie-cat, which hisses at me threateningly. "We don't know who Ms Grimm will use it on next."

"Us!" I say. "That's who she'll use it on next if she finds us here. US! Unless that scary cat gets us first." I can't meet the cat's evil gaze so I look up at the house. Black windows stare back, murky and malevolent.

"I want to go home," I whimper.

"Pull yourself together! We only have eight days left to save the world from exploding brains!" Holly waves her hand for emphasis, accidentally dislodging the zombie-cat, which miaows angrily and stalks off in search of superior prey. "As well as being dangerous in its own right, the brain ray is our best lead to the Space Rock. We have to find it."

"Why can't we just *ask* Ms Grimm if she's got it?" I say.

"Because villains lie," Holly pulls a 'dur' face. "It's part of the job description. Now, move it."

I glance at the house. "How can we be sure she's out?"

"Because we saw her drive away and we didn't see her drive back," Holly answers. "Stop being a baby."

"I'm not being a baby. I'm being a law-abiding citizen. If we can't ask Ms Grimm, why can't we ask Porter?"

"Because he's not here to ask, is he?" Holly kicks the skip. "I'm fed up with this whole 'missing' thing. I don't know whether to worry about him or hate him for joining the dark side."

"You can't hate him. He's Porter."

Holly doesn't hear my protest because she's darting across the road to press the doorbell. She runs back and we wait a couple of minutes. No answer.

"There," she says. "Satisfied?"

"Not really."

Holly points towards a gate on the right-hand side of the house. "That's our way in. You can't see from here but it's open a crack. Come on."

When I show no sign of 'coming on', Holly drags me to the gate and pushes it open to reveal a perfectly landscaped garden. Even the shed is painted and polished. The straight lines of the lawn remind me of Dad's love of stripy grass and make me feel calmer. I let Holly pull me towards the back porch.

"We can work on the lock here without being seen by the houses on either side," she says.

It's all very well to be able to work on the lock, but it doesn't look like we'll ever be able to open it.

"This is a job for Porter," I say when Holly starts kicking the door.

"Porter probably already has a key. I bet he's been in league with his mother all along." Holly kicks the door again and glares at the lock. "Grrr. I give up."

Unfortunately, Holly never gives up for long. Two minutes later she's running round the side of the house, calling over her shoulder, "Bet the windows are easier to unlock than the door."

As Holly is swallowed by darkness, a torch shines from a neighbouring window. The spotlight flicks from side to side, scanning the garden. Doors slam and voices carry over the fence. I can't make out what they're saying but they're heading this way. I race across the lawn and ram my shoulder against the door of the garden shed. It rebounds slightly but shows no sign of opening. I run at it again and again. I'm groaning in pain before it occurs to me I haven't tried the handle.

Ha. The handle turns and the door swings opens.

Feeling like an injured idiot, I nurse my arm and try not to breathe too deeply. Despite its perfect exterior, the inside of the shed smells of rust and mouldy feet. Tugging my T-shirt up to cover my nose and mouth, I pull the door closed and peer through a crack in the wood.

Two torches enter through the side gate.

Galileo! I'm trapped like a bug in a bathtub. The wall behind the shed is over two metres high. Even if I wasn't a PE-avoiding climbing-disaster, there's no way I could scale it without being seen. Holly's in a better position: if she moves fast, she can escape back the way we came. I close my eyes and decide my best option is to pretend I'm invisible.

"Hello? Anyone in here?" One of the torches has a deep male voice.

Probably shouldn't answer that.

Torchlight filters into the shed through the cracks in the walls. I dive behind a lawn mower. This is it. The end.

The handle of the door turns slowly. The hinges creak . . .

"Miiiiaaaaaaooooooooowwwwwwwwwwww."

The caterwaul is followed by a high-pitched scream and the crash of a torch hitting the ground. One of the lights goes out.

"What the heck was that?" Deep Voice yells.

"Flying jungle cat!" Female Voice fades as she runs from the shed. "Coming right at me. Huge, it was. Huge!"

"Don't be a drama queen." Deep Voice is still close. "It was probably more scared than you were."

"Then it'll need cat-therapy," Faded Female Voice retorts from somewhere over by the house. "Unless it's already dropped dead from heart failure. I'm not hanging around here to be savaged by wild animals." There's a clatter of heels, another crash, and a scream.

Deep Voice mutters something about "attention seekers" and "imaginary animals", but he doesn't hang around either.

I breathe a heavy sigh, which morphs into a yelp of horror as the shed door swings open . . .

"*Pythagoras*, Holly! You scared me half to death. You want to be careful out there. There's some feral cat flying about, attacking people."

"Yeah. About that . . ."

I stare at her. "You didn't … No … You didn't throw the cat?"

Holly nods in shame. "I hate myself. But you were about to get caught and when it leaped into my arms it was a sort of automatic reaction. I didn't mean to do it! It all happened so fast. Poor kitty!"

I should be reporting my sister to the RSPCA, but I can see the cat prowling by the hedge, looking offended but unharmed. And if it wasn't for Holly and her, er, cat-apult, I'd be under citizen's arrest right now, waiting for the police to arrive. My knees lose the power to hold me upright and I collapse on to the mower, shaking my head and murmuring, "Cat-astrophe."

Holly recovers enough to punch my arm, which still hurts from my attacks on the shed. Ow!

What next? The sensible thing would be to sit here for a while and convince the Voices there's nothing to worry about except a crazy cat, but all I can think is, 'Escape! Run away!'

Holly has other plans. "We can still get into the house and look for the brain ray."

"Are you mad?"

"Probably. I managed to get one of the windows open while you were having fun in the shed. Come, see."

She drags me over flowerbeds planted with

skin-flaying bushes and rams me through the window as if I'm mincemeat and she's a sausage-maker. Groaning, I stumble through the moonlit kitchen, crashing into an overstuffed bin before lurching into the hallway.

"Arggghhh!" I wail as a figure appears out of nowhere at the end of the hall.

It's a terrifying sight, with outstretched arms, wide eyes and bared teeth. Clumsy with panic, I trip and the figure lunges straight for me.

"Get back," I scream at Holly. "Save yourself."

Holly's laughing too much to move. "Mirror," she splutters between giggles.

Mirror? *Copernicus!* She's right. I've been terrorised by my own reflection. I try to laugh, but I sound like a cat in a bucket of water.

Holly starts searching the house. I can't focus. I keep thinking I can hear something, but everything seems quiet and calm. Until. Suddenly. It's. Not.

A key turns in the lock.

Fibonacci! The Voices are back and they're coming through the front door. No time to escape through the kitchen window. No place to hide in the hallway. No time to get up the stairs. With a superhuman surge of speed, I make it to the living room a second before the front door swings open. I stop to catch my breath – and panic. Where are the large, overstuffed sofas that would conceal a herd of elephants (and, more importantly, me)? What's with all this slimline, modern furniture? It wouldn't hide a skinny ninja.

I look around the room in horror. I'm doomed.

22

It's Curtains For Me

Footsteps approach. I fling myself behind the curtains, aware I'm now visible to anyone in the garden. The material clings to me and I'm convinced the Voices will spot the black velvet me-statue the minute they enter the room.

"Do you think they've gone?" Deep Voice is disturbingly close.

"If they were ever here," Female Voice replies. "Come on. It's one o'clock in the morning. I want to go to bed. I don't understand what we're doing here."

"I told you. I saw a light on. We should check the house, just to be certain." Deep Voice is taking no chances.

I swallow a scream as they twitch the curtain.

Bang! Kerrrrrang! Sounds like a pan smashing again kitchen tiles.

The Voices disappear in the direction of the noise.

I peer between the curtains and see Holly standing in the doorway, beckoning me towards the stairs. I shake my head violently.

"I'm going back out to check the garden again," Deep Voice declares from the kitchen.

Archimedes! I'll be framed in the window if he goes out there. Stuck for other options, I dart towards Holly and follow her across the hallway and up the stairs.

"Why are we going *up*?" I hiss. "Surely we should be going *out*."

"They locked the door behind them," Holly hisses back. "Besides, we haven't searched up here. We have to find that brain ray."

"Bonkers," I mutter. "You are stark, raving bonkers."

Taking a deep breath, I race with Holly across the wide, exposed landing between the stairs and the first bedroom door. She pushes the door and shoots me a triumphant grin when she spots the bedroom's wastepaper bin.

"This ..." – she bends to pull out a sheet of brown paper – " ... is the packaging paper they used for my sunglasses. And look, there's a sender's stamp from the Science Museum. The brain ray must be here somewhere. Maybe the Space Rock too?"

We search the wardrobes, the drawers, under the bed (shuddering at the sight of the turquoise duvet). We look everywhere we can think of, taking care to put things back the way we found them. Holly even perches on the edge of the en-suite bath and stretches up to push the ceiling panels out the way. Nothing.

"This is stupid." I sulk. "There's nothing here."

Holly opens the bathroom cabinet and makes a sound I've never heard from her before: part sob, part suppressed-squeal, and part little-bit-of-sick-coming-into-mouth.

"What?" I move closer. "Have you found the Space Rock?"

Holly shakes her head and points at the back of the cabinet door. I follow the direction of her finger and squeak when I realise that the white plastic casing is covered with *a photo montage of Dad*!

Pictures of Dad deep in thought; snaps of Dad poring over his inventions; screen grabs of Dad on the various TV shows he used to appear on. Some of the pictures look really old. In the centre of the display is a shot of two students outside a university building in Oxford.

"*Ramanujan!* Is that Dad on the right?"

"Yup," Holly says absently, staring in horror at the girl on the left. A strange-looking girl with lop-

sided features, bulgy eyes and a tiny angry, just-sat-on-a-wasp mouth.

"No!" I peer closer. "It can't be ... ?"

Holly nods miserably. "Ms Grimm!"

"I remember her telling me they were at university together, but I didn't know they knew each other. *Urgh!* The Grimm Reaper has a shrine to Dad in her bathroom cabinet. This is too freaky."

Holly puts her finger to her lips and points towards the door as footsteps approach.

Will this never end?

I slide under the bed, staring at the dangling turquoise duvet. Where's Holly? Do the footsteps I can hear belong to her or to the Voices? It's impossible to tell above the thudding of my heart.

"Don't forget to check under the beds," Deep Voice shouts from the landing.

Great. Now where? Apart from the bin, the bed, the drawers and the wardrobe, the room is bare. I'm not trapping myself in the wardrobe. No way ... Wait! There are glass doors. Key in the lock. Must lead somewhere. To a balcony? Maybe the Voices won't go out on to the balcony. Especially if I lock it behind me.

Keeping low, I crawl over to the doors and reach up to turn the key in the lock. But my hands are shaking and the key won't budge. The footsteps cross the landing. I'm taking too long. At the last minute, the key turns and I squeeze through the small gap, just as the door creaks open in the next room along.

As I try to lock the door behind me, something brushes past me and a hand presses over my mouth, muffling the sound of my scream.

"Shh! It's me," Holly whispers in my ear. "Quick, give me the key, I'll lock it."

"*Archimedes!* Holly!" I hiss when she removes her hand. "What are you? Some kind of cat burglar?"

She looks like she's about to smother me again, so I add quickly, "I mean like a skilled thief, not a pet-stealing nutter."

"I know what a cat burglar is," Holly hisses. "I

just thought if I ignored you then you might stop babbling. Now, give me the key. Your fingers are shaking."

I drop the key into Holly's hands-of-steel. She locks the door and pulls me back into the shadows as we attempt to shrink into the smallest space possible. The light flicks on in the bedroom. Moments later, the balcony door rattles. We have no cover; if they come out here, it's over. I close my eyes and sink down into a squatting position, hugging my knees.

"Locked." Deep Voice carries through the glass.

I shift my arms so they're covering my ears. I don't know how long I stay like that, but I don't hear anything more until Holly pulls my elbows down and murmurs, "They've gone."

I blink, reminding myself to breathe. "I can't take any more of this. There's no way I'm going back inside that house."

"How else are you planning to get off the balcony? Parachute?"

I glance down, wishing I had a parachute and that was an option.

Holly points to the couple coming out of the front door. Deep Voice is shorter than I expected, but that's all I notice. My attention is on the car that's just pulled up to the kerb. A distorted silhouette emerges and I can tell by Holly's sharp intake of breath that she's experiencing the same shock of recognition.

"Ms Grimm!" Holly squeaks "We have to confront her. I'm not hiding here in the shadows."

"We're not hiding," I murmur. "We're spying. You said it yourself, if we confront her about the brain ray then she'll just lie. And she'll know we're on to her. We have to keep the upper hand."

I'm impressed by how convincing that sounds. It even silences Holly – but probably not for long. My sister has two modes:

i) Attack mode
ii) Questioning why we're not in 'attack mode' mode.

I need to move fast. Calmer now, I tell Holly to unlock the balcony doors, and by a combination of pushing and scuttling, I manoeuvre her through the bedroom, down the stairs and out the back window, just as the creak of the front door announces Ms Grimm's entry.

23

Top Parenting Skills

We arrive home at two in the morning to find Porter lurking in the front garden, peering through the bay window.

My mouth curls up at the corners and my hands do a little happy dance. I've missed him. Holly's expression is impossible to read – and not only because it's dark.

She sneaks up behind him and hisses, "Lost your keys?"

He makes a shrill, high-pitched sound that helps me understand the meaning of the phrase 'squealed like a pig'.

"What are you doing here?" Holly pulls on a bramble and lets it snap back, dangerously close to Porter's head. "Trying to sneak in without us noticing?"

Porter ignores the bramble and rubs at the window pane. "I just spotted a smear on the glass."

"It's ridiculous o'clock in the morning and you've nipped round to clean the windows?" Holly sneers. "I thought you'd decided to leave us and move into your new family home."

I shake my head. There were no traces of Porter in Ms Grimm's new house. "Where have you been, Porter?"

"Out."

"Out?" I repeat. "For three days?"

"I've been at LOSERS," Porter admits, looking down at the lawn. "Even though they shut the boarding house after the explosion, some of the rooms have been cleaned up. Mr Kumar said I could stay for a few days during the holiday. I needed space to think."

"You knew, didn't you?" Holly challenges him. "You knew your mother was back."

"She never went away," Porter says. "She bought a new house with some of the money she made from LOSERS, but didn't register it in her name, so no one knows where to find her."

"7 Albion Road," Holly and I say, simultaneously.

Porter's mouth drops open. "How ...? Never mind. Okay, no one *except you two* knows where to find her."

"Why didn't you tell us you'd seen her?" Holly asks.

"Because I haven't."

"Don't lie." Holly reaches for another bramble.

"I'm not lying." Porter's moves out of prickly branch zone. "I've been to her house – many times – especially since your dad said that thing about the museum volunteers. But she won't let me in. She told me not to come back in case someone follows me." His voice wobbles and he rubs his eyes angrily.

Holly and I stare at Porter in disbelief, causing him to flush an interesting shade of red. I picture the Dulux colour chart and decide he's 'Ruby Starlet'.

"She's been working in the Science Museum," Holly points out. "She can't be that worried about being spotted."

"Yeah, thanks. Making me feel loads better," Porter mutters dejectedly.

"Maybe she's wearing some kind of disguise." Holly ignores Porter's obvious misery – she's not known for her empathy skills. "Did you get a chance to ask her about the Science Museum while she was telling you to go away?"

Porter nods. "She said she wasn't there on the day of the school trip."

"She lied," I tell him, feeling bad when his face

goes all crumply. "She's on the CCTV footage, just before the camera goes blank."

"She must have done it for your dad," Porter mutters. "She has a thing for him."

I cringe, wishing I could delete the cabinet-shrine from my mind. Curse my photographic memory.

"Why do you always try and make excuses for her?" I ask Porter.

"Why do you always try and make excuses for *him*?" he retorts.

"Touché," Holly says. "The fact is you're both idiots, and you're both far too easy to manipulate. We have to ask Dad what happened to the Space Rock."

"We?"

"Yes. We're a team." She narrows her eyes at Porter. "Even you. So stop lurking about in the garden and come inside."

"Being a team is good." I smile at Porter, not wanting to spoil the moment. "But I was asking what you meant by '*We* have to ask Dad'?"

Holly kicks the hedge as a thorn on the bramble cuts into her thumb. "I meant that Porter was right about you always making excuses for Dad. So, I'm coming with you on the next visit."

Ada Lovelace. This is going to get messy.

24

Visibly Invisible

Days Left to Save the Earth: 6

I secretly enjoy seeing Holly's nervousness as we enter the prison. I stride in confidently to take my chair, this time at Table Six. Holly drops down beside me, then stands up, then sits back down and starts tapping a frantic rhythm with her foot. If she'd shown any interest in learning Morse code with me, I'd think she was beating out an SOS call.

Vigil-Aunty puts a hand on Holly's leg and tells her to calm down. Holly puts a hand on Vigil-Aunty's hand and tells her to go and stand by the vending machine because we want to speak to Dad privately. Vigil-Aunty blows air through her nose like a rhino preparing to attack, but grudgingly gets up and heads across to the other side of the room, just as Dad hobbles into the Visiting Hall.

Holly's eyes widen in shock at the sight of him. I'm less disturbed because I've noticed something – well, two somethings – about his injuries:

- Although the bruises and the Rudolph nose are back, they're not as bad as they were last time.
- While the Neanderthugs have stopped the smiles and the high-fives, they're still giving Dad little nods.

CLUE 28

The Neanderthugs seem to be trying to teach Dad a lesson while keeping him on their side.

I put together a few clues and come up with my first theory:

(RECAP)
CLUE 10

Hell Raizah wants the moon
(because, weirdly, he's convinced it
will make him stronger) and a piece of
the moon has been stolen.

+

```
┌─────────────────────────────────────────┐
│                                         │
│              (RECAP)                     │
│              CLUE 11                     │
│      The Neanderthugs (were) being       │
│        abnormally friendly to Dad.       │
│                                         │
└─────────────────────────────────────────┘
```

+

```
┌─────────────────────────────────────────┐
│                                         │
│              (RECAP)                     │
│              CLUE 28                     │
│    The Neanderthugs seem to be trying to teach │
│   Dad a lesson while keeping him on their side. │
│                                         │
└─────────────────────────────────────────┘
```

=

```
┌·········································┐
:                                         :
:              THEORY A                    :
:      DAD DOESN'T HAVE THE SPACE          :
:    ROCK, BUT HE HAS CONVINCED THE        :
:     NEANDERTHUGS HE CAN GET IT.          :
:                                         :
└·········································┘
```

Holly is looking at Dad the way she usually gazes at Mum – as though she's the parent and he's the one who needs looking after. I try to see Dad through her eyes and decide the grey blanket wrapped around his shoulders is the main problem. It makes him look old and tired, particularly the way he has to hunch over to hold the ends together.

"Are you cold, Dad?" I ask. "Or is that a style choice?"

"This is my STEALTH BLANKET!" Dad declares so loudly the whole room turns to look, and Vigil-Aunty walks into the vending machine. "Good, eh?"

"Er, yeah ... Lovely."

Dad straightens up, no longer weary and wounded. "It's my best invention to date."

His characteristically smug tone wipes the sympathy from Holly's face. "Congratulations," she mocks. "You've invented the blanket."

"The Stealth Blanket," Dad corrects her. "In this blanket, I am invisible."

We stare at him. I wonder how to break this to him gently.

Holly doesn't do gentle. "We can see you, you stupid man."

"Holly!" I hiss.

"You can?" Dad asks. "There must be some mal-function."

"Argh!" Holly leaps to her feet. "Hasn't being in here taught you anything, Dad? Don't you feel any guilt about the brain rays? How can you still be as ridiculous as ever? The stolen Space Rock could blow up our brains at any minute and all you're worried about is some dumb invention that doesn't even work. I can't stand it. I'm not going to sit here, waiting for my head to explode, listening to you waffling on about invisibility cloaks."

"Stealth Blankets," Dad corrects her.

"Whatever! I'm done. Know-All, are you coming?"

"No," I say firmly. "We're in the middle of an investigation. I came to talk to Dad and that's what I'm going to do. If you can't handle being near him, go and chat to Aunty Vera about Han Solo for half an hour."

Holly is on the verge of sitting back down when Dad hands her his blanket. "Here, wear this. Being invisible might help you calm down."

"OHMYGODDAD!" Holly shoves the blanket at him, muttering, "My dad is an idiot. My dad is an idiot," over and over, like a mantra, as she storms over to the other side of the room and kicks the vending machine.

Vigil-Aunty grabs her by the shoulders and leans in to tell her off. Holly's violent gestures in Dad's direction suggest she's defending herself by blaming everything on him. When she's finished, Vigil-Aunty kicks the vending machine too.

"You wound Holly up on purpose!" I accuse Dad.

Dad grins.

I can't help grinning back, remembering a time when it was me and Dad against the world. Or, more often, me and Dad against Mum and Holly because the rest of the world was busy.

But things have changed. I'm on Holly's side now. I drop the smile, put my elbows on the table and stare at him. "I want to talk to you about the 'clue' you gave me. We know Ms Grimm was in the museum that day. Was she stealing the Space Rock for you?"

"I told you, I don't have the rock," Dad fiddles with his blanket.

"I know."

Dad looks up sharply. "You do?"

"Yup. That's why you're no longer Lord of the Neanderthugs. But they still think you can get it for them, don't they?"

"Nicely deduced." Dad nods approvingly. "But

I'm not admitting anything. And I know nothing about exploding brains."

"You don't have to admit it because I know I'm right. And even if you didn't realise the rock was dangerous at the time, you do now. It has to be returned to the museum fast. What will your Neanderfriends do then?"

"I have a backup plan." Dad taps his Stealth Blanket.

"You do know everyone can see you, right?" I check. "This *is* just one of your bizarre attempts to wind people up?"

"There's more to invisibility that meets the eye." Dad winks theatrically on the word 'eye'.

Before I can ask what the wink's supposed to signify, one of the guards sneaks up behind us and tries to snatch Dad's blanket. Dad squeals like a baby in a blender. Everyone turns to look and the guard backs off quickly. His fellow guards move forward, signalling the end of our visit.

"It's only a blanket," one guard mutters. "Let him keep it. He has enhanced privilege status."

That means Dad has earned extra treats through good behaviour. Why is he wasting them on a stinky blanket?

"He thinks it makes him invisible," I say, answering my own question.

"No he doesn't," the guard corrects me. "He's pretending he does. He hopes that by convincing us he's insane he'll get himself released early. We see it all the time."

I'm not so sure. This is more than fake insanity. I know it is. As I follow Holly and Vigil-Aunty to the car, Dad's comment keeps playing through my head.

CLUE 29
Dad says, "There's more to invisibility than meets the eye."

I think about Dad's research.

(RECAP)
CLUE 13
Dad was exploring how the camera lens sees things differently from the human eye.

Eureka!
Halfway to the car, it comes to me.
Ignoring Vigil-Aunty's protests, I drag Holly back

towards the prison building. "Quick. Have you got a camera?"

"You want some happy family snaps with our banged-up Dad?"

"Ha. Hilarious. Have you got a camera or not?"

"Not."

"I can't let you back in there, Miss," the man at the gate says I as I try to push past him. "Visiting time is over."

"I need to take a picture of my Dad – Professor Brian 'Big Brain' Hawkins. It's urgent. It could save the Earth."

"Of course it could. Unfortunately, you'll have to save the Earth using your special powers of photography on your next visit. He's back in the cell block now."

"You don't know that. He could still be near the Visiting Hall. I just need to get close enough to take a picture."

"I *do* know that. No pictures. Go home."

My shoulders sink and I half turn to go. Then I realise something. "You said you *know* he's in the cell block. How do you know? Can you see him on that screen?" I point to the monitor between us. I'd have thought the CCTV here only covered the gate area and perimeter fence, but the guard's eyes keep flicking to the screen shiftily. If he knows anything about computers, he might be able to access more areas than he's supposed to. It must be boring sitting out here all day. Perhaps watching the inmates in solitary confinement qualifies as entertainment?

"You can see the cells. I know you can. You have to let me look."

"I don't have to let you do anything. Hop it."

I open my mouth to argue, but Holly puts a hand on my shoulder.

"Do you have a daughter, sir?" she asks the guard.

The prison guard nods.

"What if she just wanted to see your face and a man wouldn't let her?"

The guard sighs, swears and then turns the screen towards us. "One minute," he says.

"That's long enough," I whisper in Holly's ear. "I have a theory I want to test."

"A minute would be great." Holly smiles at the guard. "You are a very nice man. Your daughter is a very lucky girl."

"Humph," the guard grunts.

The camera scans the cell-block corridor. I hold my breath, waiting for the moment when my theory will be proved by what's *not* on screen.

Fail!

There's Dad, wrapped up in his Stealth Blanket, still completely visible.

I'm wrong. I hate being wrong.

Perhaps I'm not as good a detective as I thought.

25

Turtle–Cam Necklaces

Days Left to Save the Earth: 5

I need to go back to the beginning. Everything is moving so fast I've lost track of the clues, which must be why I'm coming to the wrong conclusions. It's all about those vital moments in the Science Museum.

In search of more information, I hook up the video footage from the police station on my multi-screen computer. It comes from four different cameras:

- **THE MALFUNCTIONING 'INVESTIGATING ALIEN WORLDS' CAMERA**
  (showing a brief glimpse of Ms Grimm followed by nothingness)

- **THE HAIRSPRAYED 'MOON ROCK DISPLAY CASE' CAMERA**
  (showing fuzzy, hairspray-blurred images)
- **THE ENTRANCE TO 'EXPLORING SPACE' CAMERA**
  (showing anyone entering or leaving 'Exploring Space' via Reception)
- **THE EXIT FROM 'EXPLORING SPACE' CAMERA**
  (showing anyone entering or leaving 'Exploring Space' via the 'Making the Modern World' gallery)

I play each tape again and again, looking for something I've missed. Where was Ms Grimm during those fifteen minutes the camera was off? The footage suggests she disappeared completely, along with the brain ray. But that's impossible. According to my calculations, she couldn't have left the gallery without passing in front of one of the functioning cameras.

"We need access to the live feed from the museum's security cameras," I tell Holly and Porter when they wander in to watch the footage with me.

"Yeah. That's going to happen." Holly snorts. "Maybe they'll hand out popcorn and soft drinks too, while we watch."

"I'm guessing that's a joke? In which case we have to stage a re-enactment."

"Like *Crimewatch*?" Porter grins.

"Just like *Crimewatch*." I ignore the sniggers and google 'spy cameras'. "We'll set up our own camera feeds and figure out what Ms Grimm was doing during the 'Alien Worlds' blackout."

"How?"

"Let me worry about that. You two worry about convincing Uncle Max to take us back to London."

As we enter the Science Museum, I close my eyes so I can picture the exact directions in which the CCTV cameras were pointing on the police footage. I move Porter into the position of the camera covering the entrance from Reception and hand him one of my new Spy Cam Necklaces.

"This contains a digital video recorder with a built-in USB port for easy downloading. It captures video in AVI format at thirty frames per second—"

"It's a necklace." Porter interrupts. "You're asking me to wear a necklace?"

"Only for half an hour," I say. "Think of it as a medal rather than a necklace."

"It's sparkly and shaped like a turtle."

"Special offer," I explain. "Four for the price of two. We needed four cameras."

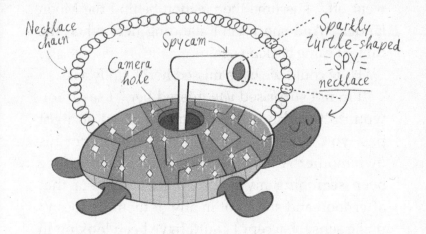

Necklace chain

Spycam

Camera hole

Sparkly turtle-shaped =SPY= necklace

"There are only three of us."

"We'll improvise," I say. "Porter, you stand here and cover the entrance. Holly, you head over there so you're filming the display case." I angle Holly so she's facing in the right direction. "I'll put one of the spare camera necklaces here, in the 'Investigating Alien Worlds' section, to represent the camera that blanked out, and the other one here, covering the exit."

"What about you?" Porter asks.

"I'm going to be your mum."

"Ugh. Talk about scarred for life."

"What I mean," I say with more patience than Porter deserves, "is I'm going to figure out how she escaped. She was standing here when the camera went off." I assume the position behind the Moon lander. "And she wasn't standing here when the camera came back on again."

"How could we have missed her?" Holly asks.

"I'm not surprised *you* missed her," I say. "You wouldn't notice if the Queen marched straight past you. But it is weird Porter didn't spot his own mother. And I can't believe I missed her. I've been searching my memory for images of that afternoon and she's not in any of them. It doesn't make sense. I accept I could have been looking in the wrong direction for a few seconds, but not for over fifteen minutes." I close my eyes and picture the gallery. I focus all my attention on the images. Where is she? Where was the Grimm Reaper when the Space Rock was stolen?

"I don't know!" a familiar voice cries. "Stop asking."

I swivel round to find Museum Curator Gnome doubled over, clutching his head. He's still wearing the same green suit, and the oniony smell coming from the armpits suggests it's not because he owns several versions of the same outfit. The suit that was so perfectly pressed nine days ago is now wrinkled and stained and the waistcoat is missing a couple of buttons.

His eyes are bloodshot and his beard contains a collection of breakfast items. At a quick glance I spot a baked bean, a Coco Pop, several raisins, and – wait – is that the tail of a sardine?

"What?" I ask him. "What don't you know?"

"The Grimm Weeper," the gnome wails. "I don't know where she is."

"Impossible! How did you know … ?" I grab Porter by the shoulders. "Did I ask where your mother was out loud?"

"Owww!" Porter rubs his arms. "What are you talking about?"

"I'm sure I didn't." I release Porter and prod Museum Curator Gnome. "How do you know we're looking for her?"

"For whom?"

"The Grimm Reaper. You said you didn't know where she was."

"I don't."

"But you know who she is?"

"No."

"Then how do you know we're looking for her?"

"You told me."

"No I didn't."

Museum Curator Gnome clutches his head. "Then it appears I am losing my rather fine mind. What's happening to me? Must be sleep deprivation. Such long hours. So many voices." His eyes roll and he starts shouting. "IT'S THE VOICES! STOP THE VOICES!"

I remember the weird conversations I overheard last time we were at the Science Museum and something clicks.

CLUE 30

Some Science Museum employees can
hear what other people are thinking.

I touch his arm to try and calm him down. "I think you're reading our minds," I say. "I think it's a side effect of the pressure the Space Rock is creating in your brain.

"STOP THE ... ! What?" He pauses mid-rant and stares at me, his eyes clearing slightly. "Mind-reading? That's ridiculous. Impossible ... And what's a Stealth Blanket?"

26

Impossibly Invisible

Holly rolls her eyes "Mind-reading? Get real! And don't start again with the Stealth Blankets."

"He's the one who mentioned the Stealth Blankets." I point at Museum Curator Gnome. "You can't have it both ways. If mind-reading is impossible then he came up with the phrase on his own and I had nothing to do with it."

"You probably hissed it at him," Holly says. "You did say you thought the brain ray and Space Rock were stolen by the Invisible Man."

"That was a joke! I don't think Ms Grimm was invisible. We could see her, but we couldn't see *her*. I think she was the woman under the blanket."

That grabs Holly's attention.

"Remember the woman under the blanket?" I ask. "She was here, beside the Mars lander. She was here, near the Space Rock." I'm screeching in my excitement, so I try to talk more slowly. "What if Remarkable Student Alexander was standing in front of the camera to hide her from view. What if she smuggled the brain ray out of 'Exploring Space' under a blanket? What if she took the Space Rock out the same way?"

Porter shakes his head. "They shut the museum down the minute it disappeared and searched everyone straight away. They're hardly going to let somebody leave the building with a blanket over their head and a suspicious-looking bulge beneath it."

Hmm. Good point.

"She wouldn't need the blanket once she was outside the room," I realise. "If she's a volunteer she'd be a familiar face. Have you got a picture of your mother?"

Holly snorts. "Of course he doesn't. She's as good as disowne— Oh."

Holly chews her lip as Porter's face turns Ruby Starlet and he pulls a photograph out of his pocket. I tell Porter to show the picture to the Museum Curator Gnome.

He recognises her immediately. "That's Mallory Trimm. But her hair's all wrong."

Mallory Trimm, Mallory Grimm. Makes sense.

Easier to fake your ID if you only change one letter of your surname.

"Do you remember seeing her leave the museum on the day of the Space Rock's disappearance?"

"No, but I remember she had to go early. To pick up her son from school."

Porter stiffens. Hard to be used as an excuse when your mother won't even open the front door to you.

"I don't suppose the guards were told to search employees as they left?" I ask.

Museum Curator Gnome eyes me sharply. "Are you suggesting I am unaware how to do my own job?"

I think hard about the vital and valuable role Museum Curators play across the globe. The gnome's shoulders relax and he stops twitching.

"Actually, my dear," he says, sounding more like his old self, "I insisted the fine officers of the London Metropolitan search our employees twice as carefully. I didn't want people suggesting it could have been an inside job."

So Ms Grimm couldn't have been carrying the Space Rock. Unless the security guards weren't paying proper attention to ... Oops. Forgot to block my thoughts.

Museum Curator Gnome glares at me over his glasses and I lift my hands in mock-surrender.

"What about a strange-looking thing wrapped in silver foil? Did you ever see Mallory Trimm with something that looked like a brain ray?" I try to picture it in my mind.

Museum Curator Gnome grabs his head with a groan. "There was something," he says slowly. "But it was days later. I discovered Mrs Trimm carrying a rather peculiar-looking turquoise machine. I told her I would have to write the incident up, but she explained she'd just found it and was on her way to hand it in to Lost Property."

"Clever," I say, as a piece of the puzzle drops into place.

The suspicious look returns to the gnome's face and he stares closely at Holly, who's clearly not thinking positive thoughts about Museum Curators. "Of course I checked she'd handed it in. I do know how to conduct an investigation, whatever you may think, young lady." His eyes do that strange rolling thing and he looks like he's about to start yelling again.

"O-kay. Time to go." Holly moves quickly, rooting around in her bag for her mobile to call Uncle Max. "This place is too weird."

We push through a crowd of cameramen, all obviously hoping to catch exclusive footage of an exploding brain. I hear one ask if it's worth buying animal offal to smear over a few exhibits. (The general consensus is that it would be hard to find anything grey and wrinkly enough to be convincing.) Another suggests using pre-existing exploding-brain images. Because they all seem so miserable, I pull a page out of my notebook and make a few helpful notes:

None of the cameramen seem particularly grateful. "No wonder nobody likes the press," I mutter.

"Forget them," Porter says. "I'm more worried about the Museum Curator."

"I fear he may be experiencing the lethal effects of the Space Rock," I say slowly.

"Mind-reading?" Porter scoffs. "Hardly lethal. Are you suggesting people's heads fill up with so much psychic information they just explode like a bomb?"

"Hardly." I laugh along with him, deciding not to admit that I googled the possibility yesterday after watching *Indiana Jones and the Crystal Skull*.

"Forget the mind-reading." Holly says. "The lethal part is that the Space Rock makes people crazy-angry."

The enraged roar that follows us out of the Science Museum supports her point.

"I think the two are connected," I tell them. "Imagine that the pressure in your brain has you hyped up and 'crazy-angry' and then you start to hear all the horrible things people are thinking about you."

"Yikes," says Porter.

"Double yikes," agrees Holly. "We need to find that Space Rock, whatever it takes. And while we're on the subject of crazy-angry . . ." She turns to Porter. "We need to talk to your mother."

27

A Grimm Challenge

7 Albion Road looks different in the daylight. Brighter. Less ominous. But still a bit ominous. I mean, the Grimm Reaper is in there.

At least the skip smells better. Someone must have emptied it. Ms Grimm probably called the council and insisted on it. She always was a neat freak. Wait! Something tells me that's a clue. An image of a moonlit kitchen pops into my head. I don't know how the two are connected, but I've learned to trust feelings like this.

CLUE 31

Ms Grimm is a neat freak.

CLUE 32
I missed a clue last time I was in
Ms Grimm's kitchen.

We walk towards the front door. It's a competition of who-can-walk-the-slowest as we all try not to be the person who rings the doorbell.

"She's *your* mum." Holly shoves Porter forward.

"Yeah, but she's already told me to go away." Porter drops back. "She hasn't told *you* to go away yet."

Holly rolls her eyes and presses the bell, but the minute we hear footsteps in the hall, she pushes me in front of her.

"Hey!" I fold my fingers into my palm to stop them shaking as I wait for the door to open. The wait goes on. I chew my knuckles. There's a peep-hole in the door, just above eye level, and I *know* Ms Grimm is looking at me.

"Hello?" I say.

Nothing.

"You try," I hiss at Porter.

He shakes his head. Fair enough. He's standing in full view of the peephole. He shouldn't have to ask his own mother to open the door.

"We need to talk to you about the Space Rock," Holly says. "People's lives are at risk."

We hear footsteps moving away from the door. I could have told Holly Ms Grimm wouldn't care about other people's lives.

"Wait!" I call. "We can tell you about the special brain powers the Space Rock gives people."

The footsteps stop. There's a sigh. And a shuffle. And back they come. The door creaks open an inch. "What special powers?"

"I'm not telling you anything while we're stuck out here on the doorstep," I say, hoping my voice doesn't wobble.

"Looks like you'll have to come in then," Ms Grimm mutters. "Quickly. I don't want anyone to see you."

"Why?" Holly asks. "I thought the police had decided there was 'insufficient evidence to prosecute'."

"I don't know if it's the police," Ms Grimm says. "But *someone* is spying on me and I can't afford to be distracted."

Holly and I exchange guilty 'spy' glances. Fortunately Ms Grimm doesn't notice.

"What can't you afford to be distracted from?" I ask. "The Space Rock? The brain ray? Both?"

"I don't know what you're talki—" Ms Grimm

breaks off mid-sentence and eyes me speculatively. "You helped design the brain ray. You must know how to fix it."

I wince. I don't like to be reminded of my role in inventing the brain ray. I had no idea at the time how badly it would be used and abused. But I've learned my lesson now. Maybe I *could* fix it, but there's no way I *would*. Still, no need to tell Ms Grimm that. I try to pull an 'inscrutable' face, but I realise I'm not one hundred percent sure what inscrutable looks like. So I add a shrug and ask innocently, "Are you saying the brain ray's not working?"

"Was it damaged in the post?" Holly giggles. "Was your super-evil brainwashing machine defeated by the Royal Mail?"

Ms Grimm gives her a look that would kill a lesser mortal. "What were you saying about special powers?"

"Nothing." Holly steps forward. "Know-All's saying nothing until you tell us what you did with the Space Rock."

"Is that so?" Quick as the flashiest flash Ms Grimm seizes Holly's wrist and twists it behind her back until Holly screeches in pain.

"Mother!" Porter yells. "What are you doing?"

"Be grateful it's not *your* arm, traitor boy," Ms Grimm snaps.

"Top parenting skills," Holly squeaks as Ms Grimm hoists her hand higher.

"Stop it!" Porter yells.

"It will all be over as soon as you tell me about the Space Rock's special powers."

"I will," Holly squeals, "when you let go of my arm."

Ms Grimm twists harder.

"Okay, okay …" Holly grits her teeth. "What the Space Rock does is … Owww!"

Ms Grimm gives her arm another wrench.

"The Space Rock helps you read minds," Porter yells. "It helps you read minds and it makes you crazy-angry. NOW LET HER GO!"

Porter runs towards Holly as his mother releases her, but stops when he sees Holly's face. "What? What did I do?"

"You told her about the Space Rock."

"But you were about to tell her yourself."

Holly shakes her head and cradles her arm.

"She wasn't going to tell me the truth, you silly boy." Ms Grimm laughs harshly. "Some children weren't brought up as well as you were." She reaches out to touch her son, then leaves her hand dangling awkwardly as she gazes at him with wistful pride. I realise for the first time that it can't have been easy for her to send him away.

"You were going to lie?" Porter asks Holly, oblivious to his mother's dangly hand.

Holly shrugs.

"Oh."

"Yeah. Oh." Holly glares at him.

"Well this has been fun," Ms Grimm trills, pointing to the door. "What a shame you have to leave."

"But you haven't told us about the Space Rock," Porter protests.

"Well spotted." Ms Grimm holds the front door open for us. "You always were an observant child."

"Why don't you tell Know-All what's wrong with the brain ray?" Holly suggests, a little too desperately. "Maybe she can help fix it."

"No more tricks." Ms Grimm picks up a broom and brushes us towards the door. "Someone else will fix the blasted machine. It's the least I deserve. Now scram."

"We're not going anywhere," Holly declares. "Not until you tell us—"

"Out!" Ms Grimm whacks Holly with the broom, then hands it to Porter. "You can stay, son. As long as you put out the rubbish first."

Porter looks from his mother to us, clutching the broom as if it's the only thing keeping him attached to Earth. "But—"

"Them or me," Ms Grimm says.

Porter looks at us and holds his broom tighter.

"It's okay," I tell him. "Stay if you want."

Holly nods. "I understand if you want to stay. But if you touch me with that brush, you die. The rubbish will put itself out."

Porter laughs in a not-really-laughing-at-all kind of way, and hands the brush back to his mother. "I choose them," he says sadly. "Because they didn't ask me to."

"I don't need a reason," Ms Grimm snaps, but with less venom than usual. She looks more sad than angry. "I certainly don't need a *stupid* reason. Go away. All of you."

She moves to start sweeping us again, but we don't need brushing. We're already on our way. Without thinking, I take Porter's hand. It's only when we reach the skip that I realise Holly is holding his other one.

The skip! The *empty* skip.

"Rubbish!" I yell, jumping on the spot. "That's the clue I missed in the kitchen."

"Y'what?" Porter says, as I pull him up and down with me.

"Your mum would never let her bins overflow." I tell him. "But the first time we 'visited' this house, the bin lid wasn't shut properly and there was something bulky inside. I remember because I stumbled straight into it. That's where she was hiding the brain ray after the Science Museum Lost Property office sent it to her. I know it!"

"We didn't think to look there."

"Of course we didn't. Everything in this case is hidden in the last place you'd look for it. That's how we'll find the Moon Rock. Think of the last place you'd look."

28

Finger Counting

"Where are you going?" I watch in horror as Holly heads for the Grimm Reaper's side gate.

"To get the brain ray."

"You can't go breaking into people's houses."

Holly just looks at me.

"That was different. She wasn't home then!"

"Seriously, Holly," Porter joins in, "Mother isn't going to let you just march in and take it. We need a plan."

"Our plans haven't worked out that well recently, though, have they?" Holly kicks Porter. "The last plan involved you telling your mother all about the Space Rock and learning nothing in return."

"My pleasure. Don't mention it." Porter rubs his leg. "I'll let her break your arm next time, shall I? Come on, Holly, the Space Rock's hardly a secret.

You only have to spend two minutes in the Science Museum to see there's some weird telepathetic thing going on."

"Tele*pathic*," Holly corrects him. "What's *pathetic* is our failure to get any information from that encounter."

"What do you mean?" I look at Holly in surprise. "We found out everything we wanted to know."

"What are *you* talking about?"

"We know Ms Grimm has the brain ray—" I begin.

"We knew that already," Holly interrupts.

"Shh. Haven't finished. We know the brain ray is broken."

Porter looks happier. "Yeah. We *did* learn something."

I nod and continue. "We know Ms Grimm has no idea how to fix it, meaning it poses no immediate danger, so no need to go bin-robbing just yet."

Holly's squishes her lips together. "Okay, I get it. No getting distracted by broken brain rays. But what about the Space Rock? There are only five days left until brain explosion apocalypse – and we're still in the dark."

"I told you I hadn't finished," I remind her. "I was saving the Space Rock for last, but since you've got the patience of a jam-crazed wasp, I'll whizz through what we learned about it."

I count the points out loud, using my fingers:

" 1. Ms Grimm knows where it is.
2. She and Dad are in contact.
3. She took the Space Rock for him.
4. Dad doesn't have it yet."

"You're just making stuff up now," Porter says.

"I don't need to. Your mother told us." I go through the points, one finger at a time.

THUMB   "She knows where the Space Rock is or she wouldn't be so keen to hear about its super powers – she wants to use them."

POINTY FINGER   "She's in touch with Dad because she said she can fix the brain ray without me, and Dad's the only other person who knows how it works."

SWEARY FINGER   "She stole the Space Rock for him, because she said she 'deserved' his help. That means he owes her."

RING FINGER   "Dad doesn't have the rock because if she'd given it to him, she'd have no hold over him. Plus he couldn't read my mind when I visited him. And the Neanderthugs wouldn't still be beating him up if he'd given Hell Raizah what he wanted."

"Excellent." Holly gives me an approving grin, her mood transformed. "I didn't realise how clever we were being! So, Sherlock, what next?"

"Shh. Wait a minute," I say as a car pulls up on the other side of the road with its windows down, news blaring from the radio. We catch snippets as the driver scans the stations for music.

"Breaking News ... Fight breaks out ... London Science Museum ... Medics called ... Museum Curator in coma ... worried he might not pull through."

Holly, Porter and I look at each other in alarm.

"What's next," I reply to Holly's earlier question, "is finding that Space Rock. And fast."

29

Blanket-Tastic

Days Left to Save the Earth: 4

I've always hated mornings and today is reminding me why. Everything keeps going wrong. First, Holly grabs the only yellow banana and shoves it in her mouth with an evil, banana-shaped smile. Not fair. I hate brown bananas. They might look similar to their yellow–banana brethren but the difference between them is huge. Two words: 'slime' and 'mush'. Then, when I ask if I can switch to the news channel for updates on the Science Museum and the Space Rock, Mum sits on the remote until we've seen the results of a lie detector test about whether the husband of some shouty woman on TV has been texting smoochy pictures of himself to other ladies. Turns out he hasn't.

Good news for everyone except me, as the news headlines have finished by the time his name's been cleared.

The way my luck's going, I'm not surprised when the man who answers the phone at the prison says we won't be able to visit Dad again this week.

"He's exceeded his visitation rights this month. We don't make exceptions, even for our 'celebrity' inmates."

"But I need to talk to him."

Prison Phone Answering Man clearly doesn't care.

Something occurs to me. "I haven't visited often enough to exceed his allowance. Who else has been coming to see him?"

"That charity woman."

"What charity woman?"

"The one who's worried about the risks facing prison inmates in the extreme cold weather."

"What extreme cold weather?" I ask. "It's April."

"Don't ask me. I told her every inmate has a spare blanket on his chair in case of cold. But she insisted more blankets were needed."

"Blankets?" I say. "What's the name of this charity?"

"I've got it written down somewhere." He rustles his papers. "Ah, here we go – 'Saving Those

Endangered by Abnormally Low Temperatures from Harm'."

"S-T-E-A-L-T-H," I spell out the acronym. "Stealth Blankets. Dad was wearing one last time I visited."

"Three of them are at it now."

"Three prisoners dressed in Stealth Blankets?"

"Not just any prisoners either. Two of our highest category inmates. Stealth blankets, you say? Hell Raizah's about as stealthy as an elephant with a bazooka."

I try to dismiss the cold chill his words give me by reminding myself that I could see Dad in his blanket, both face to face and on the CCTV camera. But then I remember the bananas. Just because Holly found a yellow one, it didn't stop the others being brown and mushy. Similar but different.

"Have you taken pictures of the men in their blankets?"

"Are you serious?" Prison Phone Answering Man loses patience. "We've got better things to do than take pictures of idiot inmates who decide to waste their privilege status by dressing up in old bedding. Now, if that's all . . . ?"

I hang up the phone and go in search of my sister. "Holly. We need to go to the prison. Now."

"No thanks. Dad will just annoy me again."

"Don't worry. We're not actually visiting Dad –

they won't let us. We're going to look at him. You can't get annoyed just by looking at him."

Holly raises an eyebrow.

"OK, fine. Don't even look at him. I just need you to persuade the guard to let us see the CCTV footage again. I think Dad has created a blanket that makes him invisible to cameras."

Holly scoffs at the idea. "He was wearing his stupid blanket and we could see him. With our eyes *and* on camera."

"Maybe it wasn't finished then ... Or worse," I realise, "maybe it was a fake Stealth Blanket, designed to lull the prison guards – and me – into a false sense of security."

"You're being ridiculous. Blankets can't make people invisible."

"Actually, they can," I say. "Scientists have shown it's possible to create a metamaterial capable of distorting the flow of incoming waves."

"Geekspeak alert. Geekspeak alert." Holly makes stupid alarm noises. "English please."

I close my eyes and picture the research I read. "It was called the Purdue cloak and it used concentric gold rings injected with polarised cyan light—"

Holly narrows her eyes and interrupts. "I wanted less geek, not more!"

"I'm trying to explain – these tiny rings steer

incoming light waves away from the object under the cloak and basically make it invisible."

"An invisibility cloak? Seriously?" Holly clearly can't decide whether to believe me or not. "Then why isn't everyone wearing them?"

"Because they only work in two dimensions – so they don't fool the human eye, only cameras. Also, the Purdue cloak weighed a tonne. So the idea was to use it to hide buildings or vehicles. No human could possible manage to lug it around ..."

"... Except Neanderthugs!" Holly's getting excited now.

"Perhaps Dad's found a way to make them lighter? He'd have to wear one, after all."

"The one he was wearing when we went to visit him didn't look heavy," Holly says.

"That's why I think it was a fake Stealth Blanket, designed to get the guards used to seeing him dressed like that. Ms Grimm has dropped new, improved blankets off since then, pretending to be from a fake charity. I need to see more recent footage. That's why you have to make the guard show us the screen."

"It might not be the same guy. And even if it is, it's a long way to go if I can't convince him."

"You can!" I try to sound confident. "And if you can't, we'll set Vigil-Aunty on them."

Unfortunately, Vigil-Aunty isn't in scary mode. She's still mooning over her missed opportunity with Han Solo Man. Porter saw her kissing the cover of the *Star Wars* DVD the other day. This is not good. I need full-power Vigil-Aunty on this prison trip.

"It's pointless being miserable about it. He'd never have kissed you, anyway," I tell her. "Because he's married," I add quickly when she lifts the Handbag of Mass Destruction. "I doubt he made a deal with his wife that allows him to kiss you."

Vigil-Aunty's scowl lessens slightly and, after I make her a cup of tea, she agrees to accompany us to the prison and even offers to pay for the taxi.

"That won't be cheap," Holly points out. "Why can't Uncle Max drive?"

"He's vanished," Vigil-Aunty frowns. "I never know where he is at the moment."

"Maybe he's gone to Lo— Owww!" I protest as Holly kicks me.

"Maybe he's gone where?" Vigil-Aunty asks sharply.

"The loo," Holly jumps in. "Maybe he's gone to the loo."

Vigil-Aunty hits us with her handbag. "If you've got nothing intelligent to say, say nothing."

Holly nods meekly.

When we climb out of the taxi at the prison, I grab

her arm. "Why didn't you want me telling Vigil-Aunty where Uncle Max has been going?"

"It's none of our business and I don't want to make her mad. Or sad."

"You think he's doing something he shouldn't be?"

"Like I say, none of our business. Come on, let's go." She points to the prison gatehouse.

Annoyingly, the guard pretends not to remember us and insists his screen only monitors the perimeter. The 'Ooh, isn't your daughter a lucky girl' thing doesn't work either. In the end, Holly is forced to resort to her traditional annoy-your-enemies-into-submission approach.

After ten minutes of the Holly horror show, Vigil-Aunty steps in. "She won't stop, you know," she tells the guard. "My niece can keep this up all day. But, if you let the girls look at your screen for five minutes, I promise to remove them straight afterwards."

The guard studies Holly, who's still hammering away on his desk, and then looks over her head as another family approaches. With a sigh of resignation, he turns the screen to face us.

30

Something Is Missing

Dad has been in solitary confinement since they showed his Neanderthug documentary – for his own protection. This means his cell is monitored by CCTV, and I have the feeling it holds a clue to the whereabouts of the Space Rock if I can just work out where to look.

I study the screen. In the left corner is a bed made of concrete. Except for the mattress. That's not concrete – prisoners probably have a union to prevent that sort of thing. Between bed and bars is a pointy concrete desk. The toilet, sink and water fountain are in the back right corner, and Dad is in the middle, pacing.

"Something is missing from the cell," I whisper to Holly.

"Your father's conscience?" Vigil-Aunty is clearly feeling better.

"It's very small," Holly says.

"Your father's conscience?" Vigil-Aunty is on a roll. Shame it's a not-very-funny roll.

"Holly's talking about the cell," I say. "And she's right. It's tiny. So isn't it weird that Dad's not using all the space available to pace?"

Dad leaves at least a metre of space in
front of the desk each time he turns.

Neither of them are listening, but it helps me
think when I voice my ideas aloud. "Also, how does
he sit at that desk?"

"Maybe he pulls the bed over?" Holly tilts her
head to one side to view the screen, as if things will
be clearer if they're diagonal.

"No. The bed's cemented to the floor. Look!" I
point to it. "So is the desk. It's not like the cell's
stuffed with furniture. Why would you have a desk
without a chair?"

"Sounds like the start of a joke," Vigil-Aunty
yawns and heads back towards the wait-and-return
taxi.

"It's not a joke. There *was* a chair. Someone said
something about chairs earlier." I wish I could
remember things I've heard in the same way I can
remember things I've seen. The memory comes to
me eventually, but it takes a while. "It was the guy
that answered the prison phone. He said something
about all the prisoners having a spare blanket *on
their chair*."

CLUE 34

There should be a chair in the cell, but we
can't see one.

"Someone must have taken the chair out." Holly
checks her watch and moves to follow Vigil-Aunty.

"Or maybe they didn't."

"What are you talki—" Holly stops short as Dad
cries out in pain.

We stare at the screen.

CLUE 35

Dad just stubbed his toe on ... nothing.

"Thankyouverymuch," I mutter to the guard and
grab Holly by the arm, pulling her away before she
can say anything.

31

Snitch?

I don't say a word in front of Vigil-Aunty, but when we get home I copy out my list of important clues and feel pretty confident of my new theory.

(RECAP)
CLUE 13
Dad was exploring how the camera lens
sees things differently from the human eye.

+

```
(RECAP)
CLUE 14
Dad and Ms Grimm were obsessed
with security cameras in the
Case of the Exploding Loo.
```

+

```
(RECAP)
CLUE 29
Dad says, "There's more to invisibility
than meets the eye."
```

+

```
(RECAP)
CLUE 33
Dad leaves at least a metre of space in
front of the desk each time he turns.
```

+

```
┌─────────────────────────────────────────┐
│              (RECAP)                      │
│              CLUE 34                      │
│  There should be a chair in the cell, but we │
│              can't see one.               │
└─────────────────────────────────────────┘
```

+

```
┌─────────────────────────────────────────┐
│              (RECAP)                      │
│              CLUE 35                      │
│     Dad stubbed his toe on ... nothing.   │
└─────────────────────────────────────────┘
```

=

```
┌ ─ ─ ─ ─ ─ ─ ─ ─ ─ ─ ─ ─ ─ ─ ─ ─ ─ ─ ─ ┐
                THEORY B
   DAD HAS SMUGGLED IN GENUINE
   STEALTH BLANKETS AND IS KEEPING
        THEM ON HIS CHAIR.
   THAT'S WHY YOU CAN'T SEE IT.
└ ─ ─ ─ ─ ─ ─ ─ ─ ─ ─ ─ ─ ─ ─ ─ ─ ─ ─ ─ ┘
```

For a moment, I wonder whether to keep my theories to myself. I've often wished I could turn back time so I could step aside and let Dad escape jail, like Porter did for his mum. Why should Ms Grimm be allowed to walk around freely when Dad's trapped in prison, being battered by his fellow inmates? (That's 'battered' like a punch bag, not a piece of haddock.)

But it wouldn't just be Dad escaping this time, would it? Three blankets = three escapees. I don't want to be responsible for Dad spending more time in prison, but I can't stand by and let him fill the streets with escapee Neanderthugs.

I slide my theory pages towards Holly. "I don't know what to do."

"Easy," she says. "Report him."

"No!" I protest. "That would get him in trouble with the guards *and* the prisoners. I can't do that to him."

"I'll do it then."

"If you do, I'll never forgive you." I shouldn't feel this loyal to Dad, but I do. Evolutionary genetics, I suppose.

"You'd choose Dad over me?" She punches my arm.

"Ouch! He's not asking me to watch you suffer, whereas you're asking me to stand by while he gets beaten to a pulp. So, I choose to have no one suffering, if that's okay with you?" I take a few deep breaths. "Besides, if we betray him like that he'll never tell us what he knows about the stolen Space Rock."

"He's showing no signs of telling us anything anyway, so I'm fine with a bit of betrayal."

Holly and I stand on opposite sides of the room, glaring at each other.

We both jump as Mum rises to her feet and picks up the phone. Oops. Forgot she was there again.

"Hello. Yes. This is Mrs Hawkins. Wife of Professor Brian 'Big Brain' Hawkins. My husband has asked me to report an escape attempt … Yes, he's pretending to be part of it so he can help bring these dangerous men to justice."

Holly and I stare at her, mouths like slack-jawed goldfish.

Mum puts the phone down and laughs at our expressions. "It was the obvious solution. This way we can prevent the break-out without implicating your father. In fact, if he manages things properly and doesn't give himself away, he could come out of this the hero."

We continue staring.

"Wow, Mum," Holly murmurs eventually. "Just wow!"

"Save your 'wows' for later." Mum drops back down on to the sofa with a yawn. "There's plenty of time for your father to mess things up. And you've still got your exploding brains to worry about."

32

Soggy Footprints

Days Left to Save the Earth: 2

The Prison Governors won't let us watch the prison break *live* because it would be a 'security risk'. But they finally agree to allow PC Eric to show us the footage *after the event*, which will feel live to us because no one's telling us what's happening.

I don't know why they're being so secretive. They wouldn't even know about the break-out if it wasn't for us. Plus it was my idea to cover the soles of the Neanderthugs' shoes with paint so the cameras could track their escape route.

The Governors have promised Dad's sentence will be reduced as a reward for (cough) *his* part in stopping the escape attempt. They've also guaranteed he'll be protected from the Neanderthugs.

"What if they don't keep to the agreement?" I snap as we wait for PC Eric to arrive with the footage. "What if Dad doesn't play along when the guards thank him for the 'tip-off'? What if someone gets hurt? What will Dad say when he realises we've ruined his escape plan? And what on earth does this have to do with the Space Rock? *Pythagoras!* This is a disaster. I wish I hadn't shared my theories."

If I'd kept my mouth shut, Dad might have escaped by now. Admittedly, he'd have released a couple of dangerous Neanderthugs in the process, but his documentary suggested the Neanderthugs are so stupid that they'd probably get caught doing something criminal and be back in prison within the year.

"Don't be stroppy," Holly says stroppily. "None of this would be necessary if you'd just let Dad carry out his evil escape plans and face the consequences."

"Dad's not evil, he's just a bit selfish and obsessed with his inventions. You can't seriously expect me to leave him at the mercy of the Neanderthugs? He doesn't deserve that."

"I don't see why not," Holly says. "He's happy to leave everyone else at their mercy by breaking them out of jail."

"That's different," I protest, although I'm not quite sure how.

"Completely different," Holly agrees. "The people on the street are innocent, Dad created his own problems and deserves whatever he gets."

"Saved by the doorbell," I mutter as PC Eric arrives with a USB stick.

I drag him straight to the computer. Time for chatting afterwards. The time code shows this was filmed four hours ago:

17:56:19 Dad, Hell Raizah and Neanderthug Number Two return to their cells wearing what must be fake Stealth Blankets (because we can see them). The other inmates snigger as they pass – but only when Hell Raizah and Neanderthug Number Two aren't looking. Both Neanderthugs are in solitary too, but I don't think they're there for their own protection.

18:00:00 The bell rings for dinner. All three men bend down inside their cells. If you look closely you can see their hands clench as if they're picking something up, and then their thumbs disappear. Hell Raizah takes a moment to grab his stuffed moon. He lifts one of its skinny arms to wave his cell goodbye.

18:01:59 As the cell doors open, Hell Raizah and Neanderthug Number Two blunder through the big puddles of paint the guards have 'spilled' outside their cells. As predicted, neither of them notice. There's no puddle outside Dad's cell. I convinced the guards it wasn't necessary as he was on 'our side' – because I knew he'd spot it straight away and complicate things by making a fuss.

18:04:02 Dad must have taught the Neanderthugs where the cameras are, as the three of them shoot past the guards to a camera-free spot in the corridor. Neanderthug Number Two swishes his Stealth Blanket a bit too early and because we're focusing on him so closely it's possible to see his forearm vanish, but if you weren't paying attention you'd have missed it. The men are not picked up by the next camera. It's a good plan, and they'd have got away with it so far.

"Why are there no guards?" Porter asks PC Eric. "None of this would be possible if there were guards watching them."

"Guards aren't considered necessary in areas completely covered by cameras," PC Eric explains. "But there are guards at every important entrance and exit."

"So how are they planning to get out?"

"Keep watching," PC Eric says.

18:05:57 The paint footprints head in the opposite direction to the other inmates. A few prisoners turn in surprise but look away quickly – I'm guessing after a fierce glare from Hell Raizah.

Again, nothing's being picked up by the cameras that would raise alarm, except the paint footprints trailing down the corridor.

PC Eric points to the screen as three men in Mobitech overalls enter the corridor. "These three were brought in to the prison to update the security system." He pauses as the men wave in the direction of the footprints. "Turns out they know your father."

I wonder if this is what Dad meant when he talked about teaching his fellow inmates 'a bit of ICT'.

18:11:49 The Mobi-tech men pull out a big set of keys and let themselves through several security doors, followed by two sets of wet-paint footprints (and presumably also by blanket-wearing, dry-footed Dad).

"Surely they're going to run into guards soon," Porter says. "Then what? They're visible to the human eye. They can't just walk out of jail wrapped in blankets."

"Dad will have a plan," I declare confidently. "He'll have invented a tunnelling machine out of a fork, a battery and some breakfast cereal."

"Dad's not in charge here, Know-All," Holly says. "The Neanderthugs are. The solution is going to be something more brutal."

PC Eric gives her one of the aren't-you-clever looks he usually saves for me.

I stare at the screen.

Three Mobi-tech men.

Three men in Stealth Blankets.

My stomach sinks. If Holly's right, I can guess what's coming next.

18:18:59 A voice says, "Hey! Look over there!"
The three Mobi-tech men look over

there. Two huge fists appear in mid-air and thump two of the Mobi-tech men on the tops of their heads. The men tumble to the ground.

The remaining Mobi-tech man turns to run. One of the huge fists reappears and bashes him on the head and then bashes the air beside him. There's a Dad-like grunt of pain.

The unconscious Mobi-tech men are dragged out of camera range by invisible hands. Bits of clothing flash across the screen as the Mobi-tech men are stripped of their uniforms.

"They're not, like, dead or anything, are they?" Porter asks. "Couldn't the guards have stepped in earlier?"

"They can't be dead," I say. "How could they confess to knowing Dad – like PC Eric said they did – if they were dead?"

"Good thinking," PC Eric says. "Although, technically, that would only require one of them not to be dead. Don't worry, though, they're fine except for a couple of large bumps on the head."

"Serves them right for helping Dad and his cavemen," Holly mutters.

"Dad didn't bop a Mobi-tech man, did he?" I ask anxiously.

"I think that was the plan." PC Eric says. "But he froze at the last minute and a gentleman named Hell Raizah was forced to 'bop' two technicians. By all accounts he bopped your father too, for failing to follow instructions."

"Good," Holly mutters as the new 'Mobi-tech men' walk into camera shot.

18:26:05   Mobi-tech Dad stumbles, clutching his head and looking around nervously. He's obviously realised their actions will have been picked up on camera by now.

Mobi-tech Hell Raizah and Mobi-tech Neanderthug Number Two, saunter along like Mobi-tech Incredible Hulks, unaware that their new uniforms are ripping at the seams.

18:29:45   A group of armed guards step out of the shadows at the next exit. One guard reaches out towards Mobi-tech Dad and grabs at what looks like the air, but must be a Stealth Blanket.

The guard flings his arms towards Dad, who disappears from view and then

reappears, inch by inch, as the guard
tugs at the air/blanket.

"Wow! You've got to hand it to Dad," I say. "That
is an incredible invention."

"Yes," Holly replies. "But look at the way he's
chosen to use it."

I nod. "On the positive side, it's helped me work
out where we'll find the Space Rock."

33

Girlfriend. Or Not.

Days Left to Save the Earth: 1

The **B**ureau **A**gainst **D**angerous **D**evices in Ireland, **E**ngland and **S**cotland (what *did* happen to Wales?) confiscate the Stealth Blankets and add them to a long list of things Dad is not allowed to work on in the future.

The police discover some half invisible prototype Stealth Blankets in the Science Museum's 'Live Science Lab' and convince the prison authorities to give Aggressive Policeman unrestricted access to Dad, to interrogate him about a possible connection to the Space Rock's disappearance.

Unsurprisingly for someone on the verge of being offered a reduced prison sentence for his 'help' in preventing the break-out, Dad is denying any involvement with the Space Rock robbery. More surprisingly, Aggressive Policeman believes him.

I suspect this is because if he didn't believe Dad, he'd have to admit he should have paid more attention to my evidence about the woman under the blanket. However, Aggressive Policeman claims he's based his decision that Dad is innocent on two factors:

i) Dad's lack of motive (Aggressive Policeman clearly hasn't interviewed Hell Raizah).
ii) Dad's failure to show any of the effects of being close to the Space Rock.

Aggressive Policeman's brains are clearly made of brown bananas if he can't see that Dad could have organised the theft without actually touching the Rock, but he's right to focus on the symptoms caused by the Space Rock.

Everything moved so fast in this case I missed a few clues. Or at least I missed the connections between them. Being smart is all about finding the connections between things.

CLUE 36
When Dad and the Neanderthugs
went missing inside the prison,
they were there and not there, both at
the same time.

+

CLUE 37
The worst symptoms from the Space Rock
have always been contained within the
Science Museum.

=

THEORY D
THE SPACE ROCK HAS BEEN 'STOLEN'
WITHOUT EVER LEAVING THE MUSEUM.

Time to hitch another lift with Uncle Max. I call
PC Eric and tell him to meet us at the museum.

"This will be your last trip, girls ... and lodger," Uncle Max announces as we cruise down the A1. "My business in London is coming to an end. Plus, it's not safe there any more."

He's talking about all the fights that have been breaking out around the city. The Emergency Services are on high alert and people have been warned not to travel into London if they can avoid it. The danger hotspots are all within a twenty kilometer radius of the Science Museum. So far no brains have exploded, and you get the impression the news crews are slightly disappointed.

The museum itself is now closed to the general public because so many staff members have been hospitalised, either with chronic head pains or as a result of injuries following attacks by fellow Science Museum workers. However, the lady who answered the phone told me there were still a few staff members watching over the exhibits and said we were welcome to pop in to investigate further as they're so desperate for things to get back to normal they'll accept help from anyone. Not massively flattering, but at least they'll let us in.

"Why is your business coming to an end?" Holly interrogates Uncle Max from the passenger seat. "Is Aunty Vera getting suspicious?"

Uncle Max keeps his eyes on the road, but they go

all narrow and slitty. "Why? Have you said something to her?"

"No, but I considered it."

Uncle Max's grip tightens on the steering wheel. "Why would you do that? You'll spoil the surprise."

Holly glares at him. "How can you be so heartless?"

"Heartless? What are you talking about?" Uncle Max turns to Holly and his car drifts across the road until a white-van driver beeps and makes gun hands at him.

"I heard you on the phone." Holly fiddles with her seatbelt, obviously uncomfortable with the conversation. "I know you're meeting another woman every time you go to London."

"Well, of course I am. How else would I get the ..." Uncle Max pauses mid-sentence and his expression changes from shock to disbelief and then he barks with laughter. "You think I'm seeing another lady behind Vera's back?" He looks almost flattered. "Wow! That would be brave. If your aunt thought I was even considering something like that she'd cut off my ... head."

"But, if you haven't got a girlfriend, what *have* you been doing in London?" Holly gazes out of the window as if the road signs might hold the answers.

"He's been meeting Mobi-tech," I announce, waiting for the explosion.

"Who?"

Okay, so that wasn't quite the reaction I was expecting. Where are the screams of horror from Porter and Holly? Where are the guilty, desperate attempts to defend himself from my uncle? Uncle Max is either a very good actor or genuinely confused.

"Mobi-tech!" I repeat. "Hello? The IT firm who helped Dad with his failed escape attempt? The guys who got bopped on the head by Neanderthugs?" I point to the bag I spotted when I clambered into Uncle Max's car. The bag with the large Mobi-tech logo on the side.

Holly and Porter gasp in shock. Finally, some normal reactions.

Not from Uncle Max though. His face takes 'confused' to whole new levels "Mobi-tech? They're just the company providing the technology."

"What technology?" Holly stretches her seatbelt and shifts in her seat to face him. "Let me get this right – you're meeting a mysterious tech-lady connected to the people who tried to break Dad out of jail?" She turns to me and Porter. "Is that better or worse than having a girlfriend?"

"Mobi-tech is a big company," Uncle Max

protests. "I wasn't involved in any attempt to release your father. Nor would I ever be! No offence … Well, a bit of offence I suppose, but not to you personally."

Holly doesn't look offended. I'm withholding judgment until I figure out what he's talking about.

"You still haven't told us what you were up to," Holly says.

Uncle Max sighs. "Can I just say these trips to London are all to do with a gift for Vera, and leave it at that?"

"A gift for Aunty Vera?" Holly smiles and looks ready to drop the subject, but I'm curious now.

"What kind of gift would Aunty Vera want from Mobi-tech?"

"Oh, look!" Uncle Max points out the window. "We're here already. What a shame, no time to discuss it." He pulls in to the kerb. "I'm just picking something up today, so only forty-five minutes this time. You'll have to move fast."

As we enter the Science Museum, I forget about Uncle Max's gift-buying cover-up. We have bigger Space-Rock-related mysteries to solve.

34

Mind-Reading

I recognize the walnut-faced receptionist immediately.

"Walnut-faced?" Miriam the Receptionist glowers at me.

Uh-oh. I'd forgotten about the mind-reading.

"Mmm. Walnuts. My favourite snack," I mutter quickly, looking for a way to distract her. "Porter, show Miriam that photo of your mum."

Porter pulls it from his pocket.

"Miriam, do you recognise this woman?"

"Of course I do," Miriam says. "Mallory Trimm isn't a person you forget."

This is true. "Then do you remember what she was wearing on the day the Space Rock went missing? A blanket perhaps?"

"A blanket? Why would a person wear a blanket?

Is this some kind of joke?" Miriam scowls some more. "She was wearing a suit. I remember because it was a particularly ugly one. Plaid polyester in green, rust and cream. Single breasted with two buttons at the front and—"

"Okay, okay, got it. Not a blanket."

So Ms Grimm must have hidden the blanket somewhere between 'Exploring Space' and Reception. What are the options?

1. The 'James Watt and Our World' gallery?
No. Museum Curator Gnome hung out there and he'd have noticed a random blanket lying around.

2. The toilets?
No. A blanket would stand out like a ... well, like a blanket in a toilet.

3. The museum café?
Surely someone would have noticed. The place is really popular. Clearly the burnt food on the day of the Space Rock's disappearance was a one-off. It must have happened when the café workers left the kitchens to answer the police officers' questions ... *leaving the café empty!*

That's got to be a clue. I can't believe I didn't think of it before.

CLUE 38
Most areas of the museum were, at least temporarily, left empty while the police officers were questioning people.

The memory of the burning smell triggers an image in my brain.

I remember the thought that went through my head on the day of the Space Rock heist, and picture it in a clue box:

CLUE 39
(Which probably should have been CLUE 7)

I've never seen a place with as much firefighting equipment as this museum café – extinguishers, sand buckets, FIRE BLANKETS, the works.

"Excuse me!" I run (well, jog, as I've never been able to run more than twenty metres in one go) to the museum café. Holly and Porter race along behind me.

"What are you ...? Ahhh!" Holly nods in understanding as I grab the café's fire blanket. "Ooooh!" she murmurs as I pull off the poorly-glued-on 'FIRE' label. "Oiiii!" she protests as I shove the blanket into my bag.

"Evidence," I mutter, unsure whether I'm collecting it or hiding it. "I have a new theory."

```
┌─────────────────────────────────────┐
┊           THEORY E                   ┊
┊  MS GRIMM GOT THE REMARKABLE         ┊
┊  STUDENTS TO ZAP SMOKIN' JOE WITH    ┊
┊  THE BRAIN RAY SO HE'D CREATE A      ┊
┊  DISTURBANCE WHILE SHE HID UNDER     ┊
┊  THE STEALTH BLANKET AND STOLE       ┊
┊        THE SPACE ROCK.               ┊
┊  THEN SHE LEFT THE ROCK SOMEWHERE    ┊
┊  TO BE COLLECTED LATER AND STASHED   ┊
┊        THE BLANKET HERE.             ┊
└─────────────────────────────────────┘
```

"What are you doing?" Miriam appears at my shoulder.

"I'm picking up something I left here the other day," I think as hard as I can. *"Something incredibly dull and not worth you paying any attention to. Now, about Mallory G-ahem-Trimm and her blanket ..."*

Miriam's face goes walnutty again. "I already told you she wasn't wearing a blanket! Just an ugly suit. A really ugly suit. Hideous. She looked much better when she popped in yesterday."

"Whoa! Yesterday? Mrs Trimm was here yesterday! Are you sure?" I can't hide my alarm.

"Positive. I remember because I had to remind security to search her. The Curator says they have to do that every time she visits. He had a tip-off."

"The Museum Curator? I thought he was in hospital?" I feel a wave of fondness for Museum Curator Gnome, who obviously listened to my warnings about Ms Grimm.

"He was discharged early." Miriam doesn't look particularly pleased about it. "Some kind of miracle recovery."

"Maybe he just had to get away from this place." Holly gestures at the miserable-looking museum staff, who are all either glaring at us or punching each other.

"Maybe he had to get away from the Space Rock," I say. "It's here. I know it is."

"Impossible! The police have looked in every plausible hiding place ..." Holly says, and then grabs her head. "Whoa! Where did that thought come from?"

"I think you might be reading Miriam's mind." That can't be good. Holly's rude enough about the things I say. I don't want to hear her opinions on the things I think.

"Too late," she grins. "You're thinking, *It's not in a hiding place, it's in plain sight!*" She turns to Porter, who's peering closely at an old jacket potato. "And you're wondering what counts as 'plain sight' and whether Space Rocks look anything like potatoes."

Telepathic-Holly is going to get annoying, very quickly.

I empty my mind and remove the jacket potato from Porter. "The Space Rock is not going to be disguised as dinner. Ms Grimm can hardly pick it up later if someone accidentally eats it, can she?"

Holly grins. "Now Porter's thinking, *Noelle can be very patronising.*"

Porter gives me an apologetic shrug.

I give him a 'that's okay' shrug as he probably has a point. As for Holly, well, I'm beginning to see why the Space Rock makes people start punching one another.

Holly just smiles smugly. "Porter is also thinking *Holly looks nice in that pink jumper.*"

Porter flushes bright red.

Fibonacci! We need to find this rock fast. All this mind-reading is causing chaos. It has to be here somewhere. All the clues point in this direction. Plain sight. Where would you hide a Space Rock in plain sight?

At the same moment, we all murmur, "Exploring Space."

35

Exploring 'Exploring Space'

It makes sense for the Space Rock to be here. It's obvious when you think about it:

- The 'Exploring Space' security guards were the first people to start punching each other.
- The staff in 'Exploring Space' were the first to show signs of telepathy.
- This is where Ms Grimm was scuttling about under her blanket.

It has to be here.

We race through the gallery, hunting high and low, setting off alarms and rattling cabinets. It's not long before the replacement security guards start shouting and moving towards us.

The Space Rock is close by, I think, as hard as I can.

If you want the pain and the voices to stop you should help us find it.

There are advantages to this mind-reading stuff. The security guards stop yelling and join us in the search.

Everyone works together. Well, sort of. The security guards keep getting distracted by the urge to wallop and kick each other but we're still covering a lot of ground. Porter, Holly and I stick to the edges of the room, away from the mad scrum of arms and legs in the centre.

I squeal as a hand comes down on my shoulder. *"Pythagoras!* Uncle Max, you scared me. What are you doing here?"

"The more important question is what are *you* doing *still here*? We were supposed to meet fifteen minutes ago. I'm not going to sit out there all day."

I check my watch. Uncle Max is right about the time. He looks cross and uncomfortable. That might have something to do with the huge square-shaped parcel tucked under his arm.

"What's in the package?"

"None of your business." In his zeal to protect his parcel, Uncle Max stumbles backwards and catches the brown paper wrapping on a missile.

As some of the paper rips away, I see a flash of gold. I stare at the shiny metallic glimmer.

The brain ray was wrapped in foil.

Was that my thought? Or someone else's? Don't know, but it's a good thought, so I'll go with it – perhaps the Space Rock is disguised as a fake Space Rock, just as the brain ray was positioned to make it look like part of the exhibition? A double bluff!

I scan the room for the best location to find fake Space Rocks. My army of mind-reading searchers are flagging and clutching their heads in pain. I need to move fast.

"Concentrate the search on the Apollo lunar model exhibit!" I yell, trying to hide my surprise when people actually follow my directions and head for the life-size Apollo lander complete with lunar landscape and full-sized spacemen. "Finding the rock is the only way to make those headaches go away. Check out any fake rocks!"

Everyone jumps into the Apollo exhibit and starts rooting around like astro-squirrels looking for space-nuts. One by one, bits of fake lunar landscape are examined and discarded. Even Uncle Max climbs in to help.

Into the chaos staggers Museum Curator Gnome. Even with a large bandage wrapped around his head, he looks far better than he did the last time I saw him. Following closely behind him comes PC Eric. And Mum!

"Mum?"

She gives a little wave as she leans on the barrier beside the exhibit, wiping her forehead and breathing heavily. The journey from car to museum was obviously a bit much.

Museum Curator Gnome joins Mum in invalid-corner as PC Eric joins the hunt.

The weird combination of anticipation, suspicion and lunacy creates an atmosphere as sticky as treacle, slowing things down and making the air feel thick around us.

"Here!" Porter yells suddenly, tugging at foil. "I have something!"

The security guards dive for him. Holly jumps up to protect him. I shout, "Oi!" several times, in my bravest voice and provide cover-fire with a barrage of fake rocks so Porter can clamber out of the lunar model display, using PC Eric for support. Slowly, carefully, he unwraps the foil and reveals ... a lump of polystyrene.

"*Fermat's* sake, Porter, you had us all excited," I grumble, leaning back against Mum, who strokes my hair absent-mindedly.

We have several more false-rock-reveals. Museum Curator Gnome kneels to examine the fake rocks alongside us. But no luck. Fifteen minutes later, the ground around the lunar model is bare, the outside area is covered in foil, and the security guards are now doubled over in pain, clutching their heads. And there is still no Space Rock.

Holly kicks the wall.

I kick myself. I was so sure this was where we would find it.

"Buzz Lightyear," Mum mutters.

Everyone ignores her.

"BUZZ LIGHTYEAR," Mum says more loudly, pointing this time.

"I think you mean Buzz Aldrin, Mum."' I turn to look at the model space person standing outside the full-sized replica of the Eagle lander. "We're trying to figure out where that rock is so could you shh ...? *Schrödinger!*" I peer more closely. "Mum! You're a genius. Look! There's something in Buzz Aldrin's hand!"

Porter moves forward very slowly to lift the small, round object from the model astronaut's glove. He holds it up to the light, gazing at it in disbelief.

"Ooooooh!" The rest of us gaze too.

There's something oddly familiar about the small, nobbly, blue-tinted rock. I track through my memory and smile when I realise. "It looks like one of the sparkly blue tablets Vigil-Aunty hangs in all her toilets."

"A Loo-nar Rock." Holly giggles. "I was expecting it to flash, or glow, or at least make some kind of sinister humming noise. Something to reflect the insane effects it's been having on everybody."

"Well, it's making my heart glow to know it will soon be back where it belongs." Museum Curator Gnome holds out his hand. "Let me see it, you wonderful boy."

Porter drops the rock into his palm, keen to be rid of it.

Museum Curator Gnome stares at the rock for long moments before clutching it close to his chest. I have the feeling he's about to hiss, "My preciousssssssss." Instead, he declares, "It's been found! The people of the world can breathe safely once more." A single tear rolls down his face. "You, madam, are a genius," he says to Mum. Then he pats Holly and me on the cheek with his spare hand. "As for you, my dear young ladies, your deduction skills are a credit to your father. Terribly clever man, you know." He strokes the Space Rock and lets the tears flow. "My reputation is saved."

Everyone is busy congratulating themselves, so I'm the only one who sees Museum Curator Gnome stop mid-stroke and turn the rock over in his hand, his forehead wrinkling.

"What?" I demand, instantly on high alert. "What's wrong?"

He shakes his head, rubbing the Space Rock's surface thoughtfully. "Nothing. Nothing. Just ... well, nothing. We should celebrate." He begins a cheer, which all the staff and policemen join in. Then, smiling widely, but only with the bottom half of his face, he runs from the room, declaring, "We need to get this back in its case."

I stare after him thoughtfully.

Holly joins me. "What's wrong with him?"

"What do you mean?"

"I could hear his thoughts. Something's wrong with the rock. But he's trying not to think about it because he's worried it could cause problems."

I remember the way he touched the rock, as if

feeling for something that should have been there but wasn't ... A part of the Space Rock missing? No, that's not possible. Is it? Holly and I glance at each other in alarm.

Before I get the chance to alert PC Eric, Mum stumbles into him, knocking him into Uncle Max, who falls against the barrier, catching the corner of his parcel and ripping the paper across the middle. All I can see is the back of the canvas, but Holly is on the opposite side. Her eyes widen and she makes a strange noise that could be a giggle, a cry or a signal she's about to transform into a warthog.

Porter moves round for a better view. His jaw drops open and he covers his face with his hands. "My eyes!"

I shuffle round to see what all the fuss is about.

Albert Einstein! Painted on the canvas is Uncle Max, dressed as Han Solo. So that's what he's been doing in London – posing for a very large, very strange portrait! But Uncle Max isn't the main feature. Oh no. The vision that has Porter poking out his own eyes is a Mobi-tech-generated, frighteningly-lifelike image of Vigil-Aunty ... wearing Princess Leia's tiny gold bikini.

"Blimey!" I say when I can speak again.

"It's for your aunt's birthday." Red-faced Uncle Max tries to cover it up, but it's too late. By now, even the most demented of the security guards have stopped punching each other to stare at the picture.

"A long time ago ..." Porter gasps.

" ... in a galaxy far far away." Holly giggles, grabbing Porter for support.

"Ha flaming ha," Uncle Max mutters.

"I think it's very romantic," I tell him.

"Glad to have cheered everyone up," Uncle Max mutters. "I thought you were supposed to be celebrating saving the world or something."

"You're right." Porter does a little waltz with Holly, then releases her and raises his arms. "I declare the Case of the Exploding Brains closed."

The response he gets is:

i) A groan from the cameramen who've forced their way in, only to discover the award-winning footage of exploding brains will never be theirs.
ii) A growl of protest from me – declaring cases closed is my thing.
iii) A rebuttal from Holly.

"It's not really closed, is it?" she protests. "What about the Grimm Reaper? She's escaped again and this time she has the brain ray."

"Which is broken." Porter dismisses Holly's concerns.

"For now." Holly says. "Plus, we think she's—"

I don't know if it's telepathy or just knowing my sister very well, but I realise Holly is about to reveal that we think Ms Grimm's taken a scraping of the Space Rock too. I put my hand on her arm and think, *Not now. This is the time to celebrate.*

Holly takes a deep breath and nods.

There may be more work to be done, but for now we link our hands together, raise them in the air, and announce together, "We declare the Case of the Exploding Brains closed ... ish."

After The End

Dad/ Prisoner 4837/ Wacky Scientist, Professor Brian "Big Brain" Hawkins ...

... is still in prison. The governors kept their promise and reduced his sentence by one month in exchange for the information about the attempted prison break. However, when it became obvious that the Neanderthugs couldn't plan their way out of a paper bag and that Dad was surprised to discover he was the source of the tip-off, they then increased it by two months. It doesn't take a mathematical genius to work out that wasn't the perfect result for Dad.

The prison officers decided he must have had inside help from one of the guards in order to communicate with his Mobi-tech allies and plan the prison break. So they're transferring him to a different prison, with a new set of Neanderthugs. The only special treatment he's been offered is access to *TV WOW!* magazine so he can make sure no more of his documentaries are shown on prison TVs.

Ms Grimm/Trimm ...

... is on the run again. Footage from the Prison Visitors' Centre identified her as the head of bogus charity STEALTH and the police would like to talk to her. Section 39 of the Prison Act makes it an offence to take things into prison to facilitate an escape, so she's in big trouble. If you add that to the continuing investigation into the child kidnapping charges from her time as Head of LOSERS, Ms Grimm must be high on the police's Most Wanted list.

After receiving an anonymous (ahem) call about 7 Albion Road, the police discovered her bathroom shrine to Dad, giving them 'love' (vomit) as a motive for her involvement. Her photograph has been shared with Dad's new prison guards and she is banned from any future visits.

Mum ...

... enjoyed her day out, but took a few weeks to recover from the exertion. Museum Curator Gnome offered her a medal for her part in solving the Case of the Exploding Brains, but Mum said what she'd really like was one of the new Wi-Fi Camera Buddy Moon Rovers she'd spotted in the museum gift shop, because it would allow her to see what's going on in other rooms of the house while she's sitting on the sofa.

After discovering Dad was no longer allowed contact with Ms Grimm, Mum agreed to speak to him on the telephone once per week. That was Porter's idea. He said Mum must still have some feelings for Dad as she had got off the sofa to help him several times. Mum says if the phone calls go well and Dad promises not to grow back the goatee beard, then maybe she'll come with me on one of my visits.

Holly ...

... has convinced Porter that she can still read minds and keeps torturing him by pretending to know what he's thinking. When she's not Porter-baiting, she is busy setting up Google Alerts so she can monitor whether the Grimm Reaper reappears. She's crosser with Dad than ever, if that's possible, but does come with me to visit him every so often: mainly so she can tell him what an idiot he is.

Porter ...

... has been far more relaxed about living with us since he saw Vigil-Aunty's birthday present. I guess it's hard to be scared of a lady you've seen in a gold metallic bikini. He doesn't speak about his mother at all, but I've caught him on my computer a few times and when I checked the search history afterwards (*not* spying – my fingers just slipped on the buttons) I found he'd been googling her name, so he must miss her.

Me ...

... Museum Curator Gnome awarded me with a 'medal of honour', but the metal has started to look tarnished already, so I wish I'd asked for a new Wi-Fi Camera Buddy Moon Rover too. Then I could send it to visit Dad in my place. Our visits have become a bit sulky since I reported his escape attempt. I'm glad we solved the case (ish), but I wish our investigations didn't always end up with Dad in prison – especially when it's me that keeps putting him there.

I told Holly and Porter it might be time for me to take a break from mystery-solving. They just laughed.

Acknowledgements

An explosion of gratitude:

To my three favourite people – Mark, Jodie and Dylan – for listening to this book while it was just a bedtime story, and for laughing in all the right places.

To the drama-tastic kids who've brought the 'Exploding' series to life in schools, libraries and bookshops around the UK and UAE: Ava, Afaranyesh, Amber, Charlie, Daisy, Darius, Dylan, Freya, Harri, Harriet, Harry, Holly, Hugo, Jodie, Katie, Maia, Maisy, Megan, Poppy, Rebecca, Ruby, Seb, Sofia, Zac and so many more. Yay, you!

To my sister Kate and my cousin Chris for prancing around the Science Museum with me, accidentally setting off security alarms, until we figured out how to steal a space rock.

To my crit. partner, Tatum Flynn, who is too funny for her own good, particularly after a few strawberry daiquiris. And to the other wonderful beings who have made this book what it is. (That may not be a compliment): Debbie Sims, Amber Dawson, Tracy Donnelly, Sue Harrison, Heidi Frost, Cousin Giles, Matthew Bage, Rachel Collier, Robert Dole, the Payne family, the very nice man at the Science Museum, and all the people I've forgotten to mention, who will be sending me grumpy emails about it soon.

To my glamorous assistants who have helped me organise school visits, book events, photos, videos and life in general – Alice (more magical than Harry) Potter, Alison Kittermaster, Gemma Hamerton, Reem Haroun, Claire Buitendag, Lydia Leeks, Sam Burnett, Hana Aziz, Svenja Cassia, Maria Murgian, Emma Wright, Roze at Horizon and the almighty Minna from Magrudy's.

To Montegrappa, the Emirates Lit Fest team & LBA Books for making me the happiest runner-up ever, and to Simon & Schuster for their all-round loveliness and for letting me share Rachel Mann, editor extraordinaire, Lorraine 'LollyPopPR' Keating, and Becky Peacock, super-efficient S&S superstar.

To my illustrator, The Boy Fitz Hammond, who should have made his name much bigger on the cover.

To the authors and bloggers who may one day explode with their own loveliness: Abi 'Moontrug' Elphinstone, Annabel Kantaria, Antonia Lindsay (thanks for the shoes), Joe Craig, Jonathan Meres, Kate Scott, Kathy Hoopmann, Liz Fenwick, Sarah Sky, Tony Bradman, Susan Mann, Wondrous Jenny, Serendipitous Viv, Minifigs Ruth, Elise, Chaletfan, Bibliomaniac, Nayu, YAyeahyeahJim, Charli, Amelie and, of course, the Book Walrus.

To Jack Cheshire and Max Dowler for added silliness, and to Elen Mulholland, Lesley Mneimne and Clare Damamme for kindly loaning their toilets to celebrity guests.

To Mrs Robinson, Mr Vipond and Mrs Foster for being my all-time favourite English teachers. And to the world's best form teachers – Lynn (without an 'e') Doyle and Kelly Wass.

And last, but by no means least, to MY MUM, because mums rule!

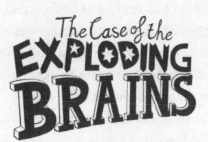

Rachel Hamilton has studied at Oxford and Cambridge and has put her education to good use working in an ad agency, a comprehensive school, a building site and a men's prison. Her interests are books, films, stand-up comedy and cake, and she loves to make people laugh, especially when it's intentional rather than accidental. *The Case of the Exploding Brains* is the second book in her series about Noelle "Know-All" Hawkins, after *The Case of the Exploding Loo.*

www.rachel-hamilton.com